THE CAMIGAS SCARF

THE CAMIGAS SCARF

Maiden

BOOK TWO

ALDER ALLENSWORTH

Edited by Robin Cain.
Cover illustration by Nupu Press.
www.nupupress.com

Copyright © 2025 Alder Allensworth
www.alderallensworth.com

ISBN: 979-8-9900189-2-1

The Camigas' Scarf

Dedicated to all of the Camigas who walk The Way.

ACKNOWLEDGMENTS

My gratitude goes out to the Camino de Santiago, the people of Spain, and people worldwide who support and maintain this magical place where the impossible becomes possible.

To Gigi Mashburn, finder of the scarf. She embodies the spirit of sisterhood. Listening to the scarf, she blessed it and sent it on its way. To Annie Herman for showing me the purpose of the scarf. And to every scarf carrier and all the women who choose to walk the Camino.

To Lorena Gaibor, Caroline Loder, and Jenna D'Amore, *(in memoriam)* who created and maintain a safe, supportive place for women who walk the Camino with the Facebook page Camigas–A Buddy System for Women on the Camino, and for graciously permitting me to use the name the Camigas' Scarf.

I especially want to thank Jenna McKenna who read the original rough draft and encouraged me to give voice to the scarf and passion to my characters. She is the glue that holds the Tampa Writers Alliance together, whose members read my drafts month after month, gently taught me writing techniques, and cheered me on when I wanted to give up.

I am honored to have the beta reader Shoshana Kerewsky who made wonderful suggestions and encouraged me to believe in the work.

I want to thank my niece Olivia Hueble who walked over three hundred kilometers of the Norte with me and showed me how a Maiden Caminos. She also helped me with Valerie's voice. I didn't want Valerie to sound like the crone I am.

My mentor, Beebe Bahrami, guided me along the way with her knowledge of the Camino and the sacred feminine. I leaned hard on her Moon guide for the Camino de Santiago.

I would have been lost without the Village to Village guide by Anna Dintaman and David Landis, and the Wise Pilgrim App.

Not just women have touched this book. Ron Angert read the first complete draft, corrected my punctuation, and my memory of key places along the way. He encouraged me to explore the Black Madonna.

I have deep admiration and gratitude for Katova, who read my tarot cards in Maariz and offered me profound guidance. She is a true medicine woman, tending to the land around her farm and nurturing the pilgrims who find their way to her home. I purchased her deck and instruction book in Santiago, and it has become a treasured source of ancient Galician lore for this book.

Four women jumped in to make this book possible and bring it to life when I was at my wits' end with revisions: Robin Cain and Geri Espy for their astute suggestions and editing,

Kim Narenkivicius for the beautiful layout, and Nupu for creating the cover with her art.

To Ben Ritter who supports my dream of making this trilogy a reality and cheers me on when I walk the Camino de Santiago.

To LifeWave technology for keeping this old body moving and quickly recovering on the Camino Norte.

And most importantly, *the scarf...*

INTRODUCTION

The Camigas scarf has been passed from Camiga to Camiga in solidarity with their pilgrimages. A Camiga is a term coined in 2015 when a few women got together to support women on the Camino. "Ca" stands for Camino, and in Spanish, "amiga" – for female friends.

The Camino de Santiago is one of the few places in the world where a woman can go, walk alone on pilgrimage, and feel safe. In March of 2015, the unthinkable happened. A young woman was assaulted and murdered. The perpetrator was found and convicted. The Camigas-A Buddy System for Women on the Camino Facebook page was created so women who want to participate in the pilgrimage have a safe place to connect with other women and plan their Caminos. At this writing, the Facebook page has over 37,000 members.

I have so much gratitude for Lorena Gaibor, Caroline Loder, and Jenna D'Amore (in memoriam) for seeing the need women have for a buddy to embark upon such an arduous pilgrimage. They have given me their blessing to use the term "Camiga."

The origin of the scarf goes back a little bit further. The story began in 2010 when Gigi walked the Camino Frances from St. Jean Pied de Port, France, to Santiago de Compostela, Spain. Along the way, she met a young American woman in a small town who was working in Spain as an au pair. The young woman was so happy to hear English being spoken she joined them for the evening. She missed the last bus back to her employer's house, but Gigi made sure she had a safe place to stay. The next morning, she left early to catch the bus and left her scarf behind. Gigi rescued the scarf and carried it with her, hoping to connect with the young woman again, but unfortunately, this never happened.

Fast forward seven years to the fall of 2017, when I was getting ready to walk my Camino. I worked with Gigi and asked her if we could have lunch. I wanted to learn all I could about the Camino before I left. Gigi brought me three gifts: a palm frond cross that had been blessed, four euros to buy a cup of cafe con leche, and the scarf.

As Gigi was preparing for our luncheon, she opened the drawer where she kept her Camino gear and hiking clothes. In the back of the drawer was the scarf. She pulled it out, and as she stroked its soft fibers, memories of her Camino came flooding back. She got the distinct feeling that it needed to go back to the Camino, but she didn't know why. She knew she had to give it to me to take back.

Gigi has the reputation of being "connected" to a higher power. I was not going to question her wisdom. I took the scarf and completed the entire five hundred miles of the Camino Frances (the Way) with it around my neck in October and November of 2017. I appreciated the warmth of the scarf as fall turned into winter. The Camino wasn't easy, but knowing

I had the support of the other Camigas, Gigi, and the scarf, I made it to Santiago.

Annie, a woman from my local area, saw me posting about my Camino on the Camigas Facebook page. She messaged me and asked to meet for lunch so I could assist her in preparing for her Camino. I took my pack loaded with everything I had carried. Sharing the contents item by item, I reminded her that less is better since she would have to carry its weight across her journey in Spain.

I pulled out the scarf and told her its story. She leaned in and met my gaze; it was written all over her face that she wanted to take the scarf back to the Camino. Reluctantly, I offered her the scarf. She accepted immediately. It was hard releasing this bit of yarn. The scarf served me well. It was around my neck the morning I walked into the square in front of the Cathedral in Santiago, completing my five-hundred-mile Camino. The scarf had been my constant companion and support. It held all the fun memories and the hardships. But what was I going to do with a scarf in Florida? So, I handed it over.

It was wonderful following Annie and the scarf on her Camino. I cheered her on with the power of the internet. Seeing pictures of her standing in front of the cathedral in Santiago wearing the scarf, I knew it had found its purpose and why it had to return to the Camino.

Annie's friend, Donna, was getting ready to walk the next year, and Annie passed the scarf on to her. As of this writing, the scarf has accompanied Camigas on sixteen Caminos.

Each Camiga passes the scarf on to a woman who has been called to walk one of the ancient paths to Santiago, continuing a tradition of support for women and pilgrimage.

The Camigas Scarf Trilogy follows the journey of three women: a mother, a maiden, and a crone. Each character is fictional as I could not do justice to the experiences of the Camigas who have carried the scarf. I did not want to intrude upon the scarf carriers' personal reasons for walking the Camino.

Women of all ages, races, cultures, religious persuasions, and backgrounds walk the Camino for various reasons. The Camino is a place of reflection and growth. The experiences of each character in the book were created in my imagination and consolidated from my interviews of women on the Camino, reading stories, Facebook posts, and my own Camino experiences. Any similarity to a real person is just a coincidence.

Each book highlights a different Camino route. The historic places each woman experiences are authentic to that particular route. I have taken care to research each route, as well as having walked them myself. Some of the albergues have changed their names and owners and may not be found on the Camino today. The information on the dog in this story highlights some of the challenges people face when they bring their pet to the Camino.

Book One – Join Helen, the mother, as she embarks upon a life-changing pilgrimage, starting in St. Jean Pied de Port. She struggles across the Pyrenees to Santiago de Compostela to discover a light within herself.

Book Two – Valerie heads to Spain to walk the last one hundred kilometers of the Camino de Santiago, seeking to heal her fragile heart. A chance encounter with mesmerizing blue eyes leads her off course to the rugged 833-kilometer Camino del Norte.

Book Three – Dorothy, our wise crone, burdened by grief after losing her husband and worn down by life's responsibilities, embarks on a solitary journey up Portugal's west coast to Santiago de Compostela. Much to the dismay of her adult children, she discovers that at the age of seventy-five, she's far from too old for adventure and romance with a modern-day Templar.

It's fun to be part of the "sisterhood of the scarf." It has become part of my Camino journey. The scarf carried me through the Frances at the age of sixty. I was called to do the Norte at sixty-seven, and I hope to walk the Portuguese at sixty-eight and write about Dorothy's journey. LifeWave photo biomodulation technology has given me the energy, strength, stamina, and focus to complete these routes and write these books. I was able to share them with pilgrims to relieve their pain without drugs and side effects to keep them walking.

Thank you for following the scarf's journey. If you've never walked a Camino, I hope this trilogy inspires you to embark on this life-changing pilgrimage one day. And if you have, may this trilogy inspire you to cherish the memories of your journey forever.

BOOK II

DANCE LIKE THE MAIDEN

Valerie

SPRING / SUMMER

Love like the Mother
Dance like the Maiden
Think like the Crone

- Stenciled on a jar of homemade Sangria
that was given to me by a wise crone.

CHAPTER I

MADRID TO PASAJES

As soon as Chase and I step off the plane, we connect to the airport Wi-Fi. I raise my phone and quickly snap a selfie reel, the "Welcome to Madrid" sign behind me, careful not to include Chase in the frame. "I'm safe in Madrid, Spain. Now off to the train."

That should do it. I hit 'Post,' fulfilling my promise to let everyone know I've arrived. Next, a quick message to Mom on WhatsApp.

The Camino. I'm here. I'm really doing this. I take a deep breath, roll my shoulders back, and try to convince myself it's actually possible.

After watching the *I'll Push You* movie in church, I just knew I had to go. What did Helen, an older student in my nursing cohort, say? "I was called."

The movie showed two best friends traveling the ancient pilgrim's route from southern France to Santiago de Compostela. One of the friends was disabled and in a wheelchair, and his best friend pushed him five hundred miles to Santiago.

The movie touched me. It gave me hope to walk my own pilgrimage, even with a heart condition, to test myself. If a guy in a wheelchair can do it, I can too.

Chase smiles at me as I finish my post to Mom. "Do you have cell coverage here in Spain?" The smile makes his blue eyes sparkle, and my heart does flip flops—and not because of my cardiac history, either. He just happened to be seated next to me on the plane. We clicked immediately. Mom said she knew Dad was the one the first time she met him. Is that happening to me too?

I stroke the scarf around my neck. Its warmth feels like a confirming hug. Helen gave it to me. She wore it on her Camino and told me the Camino provides. I look at Chase. She sure wasn't joking.

"Do I need a cell coverage plan?" I say, trying to keep my voice normal when the sparkle in his eyes creates a fire in my core.

"It'd be a good idea if you want to make calls, use data, and not spend a fortune."

"How do I get one?"

"Let me see your phone." He looks at the settings and tells me I can sign up for an e-SIM. He sets it up, and I give him my credit card to pay for it. Then he shows me how to use it and access my Spanish number.

"Thank you." I smile at him.

"No problemo. I use it all the time for work."

"What do you do?" We talked for hours on the plane but never about our careers. Just our dreams of adventure and the Camino.

"I'm an influencer. I have over twenty thousand followers, and it's growing all the time."

"I guess I'd better follow you too." I wink at him as we merge into the crowd, making our way toward the exit and the train station. OMG, all I'm doing is smiling at him. What a dork. He guides me towards a kiosk where we purchase tickets to San Sebastian, the closest train station to Irún. I'm committed.

I hear the train before I see it, and we join the passengers at the platform's edge. The crisp, cool air is nothing like the humid heat I left behind in Florida. It's tainted with the smell of diesel and the musty odor of the crowd forming on the platform. Not wanting to get separated in the crowd, I move close to him, unable to say anything over the squeal of the brakes as the train slows down beside us. I securely fasten my pack around my hips and tie the scarf around my neck. I don't want to lose anything. We politely let the passengers off. As I go to board the train, a man shoves past me, almost knocking me off my feet.

Chase steadies me, saying, "That was rude."

"It happens to me a lot. Being a woman and Black means I'm invisible."

"Really? I see you just fine."

I look up at him, gratitude flows from me, and my silly heart goes into full gymnastics. It's real. I'm going to Irún with Chase and not to Sarria, as everyone, including my Mom, believes.

I don't know how I'm going to tell her about the change of plans.

I don't know how I'm going to tell her about Chase.

We put our packs in the overhead compartment and take our seats. Chase's head comes to rest on my shoulder, and I glance over at him. He's sound asleep. That was fast.

I should sleep too. I've had very little since I left Tampa, and we start walking tomorrow. Being careful not to disturb him, I lean my head on the rest behind me and close my eyes. I'm certain the rhythm of the wheels on the tracks will lull me to sleep.

·   ·   ·

The train glides to a stop at the station, and the sudden stillness pulls me from sleep. I stretch, shaking off the grogginess. Seven hours have passed in a blink.

Chase smiles at me. "Sorry, I totally conked out. Did you

get any sleep?" He stretches, too. His toned, tanned torso is on display. My eyes trail the fine hairs disappearing beneath his shorts, and for a moment, I forget to answer.

"I did." I take a deep breath and release it, then move my neck in circles so he won't notice where I am looking.

We stand. Chase reaches into the overhead compartment, hands me my pack, and I shoulder it. He puts his on and takes out his phone. He enters the name of the local sporting goods store and uses the app to navigate. He says we have to take a bus to the store and then back to a stop close to our albergue. What an adventure—plane, trains, and feet.

Chase takes me to the sporting goods store to buy hiking poles. I wander around, comparing it to the sports store back home. It has everything I could need and more. Helen said I shouldn't take "just in case" stuff, and she was right.

We walk over to a rack of hiking poles. Chase says they're necessary, and he'll teach me how to use them. Helen had also suggested this, so there must be some merit to it. I look for the cheapest ones. Pulling two off the rack, Chase shows me how to adjust them for my height.

He checks the ends of the poles. They are pointed metal spears. He pulls a small package of rubber tips off the rack. "You'll need these on the roads and sidewalks, or you'll annoy the hell out of other pilgrims with the clicking."

I gather my purchases and check out.

Leaving the store, he inputs the address of our albergue. Our albergue, the pilgrim's hostel, is located in the town of Irún. We take the bus into Irún and then walk a couple of kilometers. The bus drops us at a busy street corner lined with shops on both sides. There is everything I may need here.

We follow the map through town and approach a roundabout, turning right where a line of people with backpacks has formed beside a chain-link fence. They must be pilgrims. We join the line, hoping to secure two beds for the night. There are about twenty people ahead of us, but Chase's guide app indicates that the albergue has sixty bunks, so we should be fine.

A young woman in front of us turns to me and introduces herself and her boyfriend. I smile at them. Chase and I aren't the only unmarried couple out here. They're going to walk the 833-kilometers to Santiago. The older couple in front of them join the conversation and let us know they're only going to Bilbao. They're from the Netherlands and spend their vacations walking Caminos.

It's finally our turn at the front of the line, and Chase pays in cash for both of us. It's only ten euros for the night and two euros for breakfast. This'll work. A volunteer takes us up the stairs and shows us where to put our poles and hiking shoes. They are not allowed in the dormitory. She shows us through a door to a room full of bunk beds. We chose bottom bunks next to each other. My bunk has a little shelf with a plug—perfect for charging my phone. That's a win. Clean clothes, my only other set, come out of the bag, and it's off to the community bathroom. There's a long trough-style sink stretched along one wall. A guy is already there, splashing water on his face under one of the faucets. A shower stall opens up, and I slip inside. There's a hook on the door—thankfully—to hang up my clothes and keep my stuff off the wet floor. Somehow, I manage to shower and change without soaking everything. Small victories.

From the next stall, Chase calls out, asking if I can take his dirty clothes. A bundle comes sailing over the top of the door. Everything—his and mine—goes into the string bag Helen gave me. It's meant to be a laundry bag, grocery bag, and daypack all in one. She swears nothing should serve just a single purpose.

The laundry room is easy to find. Two sinks. One is already in use by the older woman I met while waiting outside earlier. I claim the other and start washing our clothes by hand, using shampoo from my little travel bottle—as there's no detergent available.

"Oh, look, a spinner," she says as she puts her clothes into a basket with slots inside a bucket.

"A what?"

"A spinner. Not all albergues have them. This is great. Just put your wet clothes in it, push this button, and it will spin the water out, so they'll dry faster on the line."

I do as she suggests, then take the clothes out to the line. It's the least I can do for Chase. He's been amazing.

Chase and I meet in the common room and wander down the street to find a late lunch in town. In Spain, lunch usually ends at two p.m., then there is nothing available until after eight p.m. We spy a small cafe, the K-2, and it's open. My stomach rejoices. We only had a sandwich—they call it a bocadillo—on the train. The pilgrim's meal at the cafe has three courses, comes with wine, and costs 12,50 euros.

"Let's split a pilgrim's meal," Chase suggests.

"That'll help my budget."

Chase reads the menu. "Let's get the *ensalada mixa*. It's a salad with eggs and tuna. Then we'll have the chicken breast with potatoes and flan for dessert. They always bring bread and wine."

"Perfect." I sigh in relief. I'd been ready to open up my translation app. It's so nice to travel with someone who knows their way around.

Chase suggests that I get this bill since he paid for the room. That's fair. I pull out my credit card and pay.

. . .

I had caught Chase giving me the old up and down when he paused at my row on the plane, looking for his seat. When a man does this to me, I put them into one of two categories: creepy or not creepy.

I watched him put his backpack in the overhead compartment beside mine. When his T-shirt rode up, he took the opportunity to show off a little of his six-pack. This guy is ripped and knows it.

I deliberately ran my gaze up from his abdomen to his face. He had a beautiful golden tan, making his blue eyes even more intense. His long, wavy, bleached blond hair was pulled back into a man bun. I judged him to be at least 6'2". Nice. Standing at 5'10", I like a tall man.

Moving my gaze back down, I took in his hiking shorts and long, strong legs. His broken-in hiking boots led me to believe he was the outdoor type. I decided he wasn't creepy; he was hot.

I smiled at him when his eyes settled on my face. As a flood of blood rushed to my face, I tried to get a grip.

"Chase," he said as he stuck out his hand.

"Valerie," I replied. His grip was strong, his hand felt callused as it enveloped mine.

"Camino?" he asked as he gazed at my backpack.

"Yes, you?"

"Yeah. The Norte. It's a beast, and the surfing is dope. You?"

"Sarria to Santiago."

He looked me up and down again. "That's for amateurs. You have some long, strong legs, you'd eat up the mountains, and you need a challenge. Join me on the Norte."

"Amateurs? It's one hundred kilometers. That's like sixty miles. I've never done anything like this before in my life."

"Well, you must do something to stay in shape," he said, taking the opportunity to look me over again. I squirmed.

"I run track, the hundred," I said as if that explained everything.

"You do look built for speed and have the right equipment." He winked then pointed at my backpack in the compartment next to his.

He was such a flirt.

Though I must admit, it felt good to be noticed. He sure knew the right things to say.

"I didn't mean anything offensive by that," he said, misreading my discomfort. "I just meant you look strong enough to take on a bigger challenge."

He spent the entire nine-hour flight persuading me, chipping away at my hesitation until I finally agreed to join him on the Norte. I knew this could go one of two ways—either it was fate unfolding exactly as it should, or I was on the fast track to a broken heart.

· · ·

Back at the albergue, the dorm room is packed—twenty people must be crammed in here, which is probably why it smells stuffy. A quick scan reveals no windows to crack open, so I guess that's something to get used to. Taking out my phone, I ask if I can take a photo, pointing to it for those who don't speak English. Seeing smiles and a thumbs up, I snap the picture. It'll be fun to post.

The bathroom has this weird trough sink, which gets a pic, too. Down in the common room, a guy's strumming a guitar. This is so dope.

I sign into the WiFi and post my pictures on the Camigas Facebook and Instagram pages, careful not to post anything that will give my location away.

Opening my WhatsApp, I call Mom. "Hey, Mom, I'm here and safe."

"Valerie, it is so good to hear your voice. I only have a minute; I'm at work."

Glancing at my watch, I realize it's only three p.m. there. "I forgot about the time change. I'm still on Florida time and feeling wired."

"How is it so far?"

"It is beautiful, and people are so nice," I smile, thinking of Chase. "I'm at an albergue, have washed my clothes, and am about ready for bed."

"Sleep well, darling, and thank you for checking in. I love you."

"I love you, too." Hanging up, I breathe a sigh of relief.

Out by the clothesline, the laundry's dry. I grab it and take Chase's stuff to him. Who knew I'd be washing men's boxers? Tucking my clean clothes into my pack, I crawl into bed. Sleeping in tomorrow's clothes makes things easier anyway. I look at the smiles in the picture I snapped, bringing a smile to my face. Snuggling down into my sleeping bag, content, I thank God for my first night on the Camino.

. . .

Other people stirring wakes me up. It's still dark in the room. I look at my phone. It's six-thirty a.m. Groaning, I roll back over and bury my head in my pillow. Suddenly, something soft hits the back of the head. I sit up, and Chase is grinning at me. I toss the pillow back at him and pull myself out of bed. We head down for a simple breakfast of coffee and toast with jelly. Chase suggests I make a jelly sandwich for the road. We take care of our morning toilet. I can't get over the water trough. It's so weird, but it works. There are four of us strangers brushing our teeth at the same time. After we get our packs ready, we shoulder them, tie up our boots, and head out.

Chase points out the first yellow arrow as we follow the older couple down the road and around the roundabout. The arrows take us through town and over a tidal creek where small, colorful fishing boats rest on its bank. Chase tells me that these yellow arrows, either painted on roads, telephone poles, rocks, or sometimes even embedded in an official concrete marker, will guide us across Spain to Santiago de Compostela. The road suddenly turns and goes straight uphill. It's only wide enough for one car.

We're walking beside pastures on one side of the street and nice houses on the other. In one pasture, there's an absolutely adorable cow and calf. I pull out my phone to take a picture, but a honking horn catches my attention. A truck is trying to get down the road, and a car is making its way up. This is going to be interesting. Chase and I flatten ourselves next to the fence, corralling the cow and calf. The cow moos in protest.

"I'm not going to hurt your baby," I say to reassure her.

The car backs down into a drive and lets the truck, which has an emblem of a plumber on the side, go by. That's right. These people are going to work. I'm so blessed to be able to take the time to go on this incredible journey.

We continue along the road and arrive at an old church surrounded by a stone wall. Consulting my guide app, which Chase helped me download last night, I discover that the church is the Santuario de Guadalupe, built in the sixteenth century to protect the surrounding area. Pilgrims in the churchyard appear to be taking a break. I glance at the pedometer on my phone; we've walked about four kilometers so far. I'm grateful for a break. I can feel my breath getting a bit short, and my heart is beating too hard as I try to keep up with Chase. I don't want to appear weak.

We drop our packs by a picnic table and pull out our jelly sandwiches for a snack. I sit down and do a self-check. My breathing and heart rate are normal. That's a relief. After eating, I wander into the church. There's a table in the back where pilgrims put a stamp on their credentials. I pull out my credential and get my second stamp. The first was last night at the albergue.

I'm doing this. I'm a pilgrim.

I walk up the aisle towards the altar. "Oh my God. She's black like me," I say out loud.

Chase walks up beside me. "And...?"

I move closer to the altar. The statue of the Madonna is the predominant figure in this church. She's carved out of wood and standing behind the altar on a pedestal. Glowing in a golden gown with a red cape, she holds a black baby Jesus on her left hip and a golden scepter in her right hand. There's a gold crown on her head and a silver halo of stars above her. She's stunning. I've always seen the Madonna portrayed as a white woman with a white baby Jesus dressed in blue robes. I've never heard of her being black.

I bow my head in respect and move backward until my legs touch the front pew, then I sit. I stroke the scarf wrapped around my neck, blessing Helen for giving it to me and encouraging me to take this pilgrimage. It's so crazy. Just two days ago, I was only planning on walking one hundred kilometers. Then I meet a man on the airplane who convinces me to walk the eight hundred kilometers of the entire northern route with him. And today, at the very beginning of this adventure, I see a statue of a black Madonna. It's a sign that I'm where I am meant to be.

Chase takes a seat beside me. "What color did you expect a Middle Eastern woman to be? Europeans made the Virgin Mary white for propaganda. They figured white people would only buy the virgin story if she were made to look like them."

"What makes you think white women have the niche on virginity?"

"Well, we, particularly white men, do have a sordid history of using women of color for our sexual pleasures while white women are for marrying."

"Humm. I never thought of it that way. Some men do look at me in a way that gives me the creeps. Is it my skin color? I thought all women were looked at as vehicles for pleasures by men."

"Can you fault us for that?" He grins. "But there are gradients. You have brown skin and a great body, but you give off conflicting vibes. There's the 'Don't mess with me' and the 'Take care of me.' Not an easy read." He winks. "I saw you looking at me too, by the way."

I blush and walk back out to the churchyard. Chase follows, and we shoulder our packs. We leave the churchyard and find the next arrow on a guard rail, pointing us up the road.

We stop at an overlook and see surfers far below us riding the waves. Breathing deeply, I wish I was down there with them instead of up on this mountain. We don't have mountains in Florida. This is my first, and I'm not sure I like it. Going up makes my heart race. I have to be careful. I glance over at Chase. He's already started walking.

The next yellow arrow points to a dirt path leading into the woods. Chase turns, and I follow. Soon, an information sign gives us two choices: go up over the mountain or take a lower path around the side of the mountain. Chase doesn't hesitate and immediately starts up the mountain path. A man is talking to the elderly couple who started with us this morning, trying to dissuade them from taking the mountain route. He tells them how challenging it is. The older man scoffs at him, then he and his wife start up through the boulder field on a narrow dirt path. If they can climb an eighteen-hundred-foot mountain, so can I, even if it kills me.

I hardly make it twenty feet before my heart feels like it is going to explode. I find a place to anchor myself by sticking my poles into a patch of dirt between two boulders and I stop. My mind races as quickly as my pounding heart. This is crazy. I was afraid this would happen. I overestimated my abilities.

I was born with a hole in my heart. Surgery corrected the defect, but I've been under the care of a cardiologist ever since. Mom didn't think I could handle doing a pilgrimage of this magnitude and she still thinks I'm just walking the flatter route from Sarria to Santiago. She's going to be pissed when she learns where I am and what I'm doing. I should have listened to her.

I let a pair of sparkling blue eyes, and a hot bod charm all semblance of reason away. What if my heart ruptures and I die right here? The police will call her from northern Spain and let her know I've died on a mountain, just like in the movie, *The Way*. No one even knows where I am in Spain. What a fool, following a man against my better judgment.

"Come on, Valerie," Chase calls out above me.

I have two choices: down or up. I'm not going to let him see me sweat. Starting up again, I pick my way among the boulders. A yellow flowering bush peeks from between the outcroppings. I'm not familiar with this plant. I take a picture and catch my breath. Ah, what a good excuse to stop and breathe. Climbing once again, I make it to the final outcropping of rock. Chase reaches for my hand and pulls me up the last steep step.

"Worth the climb." Chase smiles. His blue eyes twinkle, and the sun sets his gold hair on fire. He puts his arm around my waist and leans in for a kiss. As I lean in towards him, there's a backward tug on my neck. The end of the scarf has caught on one of those yellow bushes. I free it and turn back, but the moment has passed.

A huge meadow opens up before me, with a path along the ridge line in the middle. The meadow is covered in tiny white flowers with yellow centers. I bend down for a closer look—fleabane. We have this flower at home. We cook it like sautéed spinach to remove the hairs. Mom also keeps it in sachets to ward off insects.

An entire herd of horses is grazing, and foals are playing. The meadow must provide them with all the nutrients they need. Can I get close enough to pet one?

The view over the edge of the cliff on my right is the amazing turquoise blue of the sea. On my left, a valley with fields looking like a miniature checkerboard, interspersed with tiny villages. I am amazed at how clean the air smells. There is nothing to pollute it. If my heart explodes now, I'll die a happy girl.

He smiles and says, "Let's get moving. We aren't at the summit yet."

The gentle incline to the summit is scattered with old ruins. The elderly couple is making their way up the dirt path. They are tiny in the distance. We have a long way to go, yet I can't help but take my time and enjoy this landscape.

A mare and a nursing foal that could have been born this morning are standing beside the path. I approach slowly to take a picture. The mare eyes me with suspicion. I stop so I don't spook her. How precious. These horses look wild. There are no fences, but someone must care for them up here. I'd stay here and care for them.

We continue up the ridge line to the summit, recognizable by the radio towers reaching high into the atmosphere. Resting on some rocks at the base of the towers, Chase pulls two apples out of his backpack and hands me one. I have water but didn't even think about food besides the jelly sandwich. We still have over eight more kilometers to walk before we get to the next town.

A poster in the albergue last night read, "The Pilgrim Appreciates. The Tourist Demands." I'm a pilgrim. I smile at Chase in gratitude, my heart flutters for an entirely different reason.

We begin the descent into Pasajes and stop at a bar by the river for lunch. Chase orders a tortilla. He explains that it's an omelet on steroids and will give us the protein and carbs we need to make it to San Sebastian. I order one too.

It's full of potatoes and onions and made in a round pan, like a pie. It's cut into generous slices and served cold with bread. He also orders two Aquarius for us to rehydrate and replenish electrolytes. I love that he is so health-conscious.

When I stand up, I am stiff and sore, but my energy is better. I shoulder my pack and follow Chase to a dock. He explains that we have to take a ferry across the river to continue along the way. The river is huge, and there are freighters. I can hear the clanging of industry in the port. Disembarking on the other side, we follow the river towards the sea.

The sidewalk ends at a set of steps carved into the side of a cliff. Chase starts up. I glance around for another way to go, but there isn't one. I start climbing. As the stairs switch back, the handrail disappears. I can't see the top ahead. My breath quickens, and my heart is pounding. A wave of dizziness envelops me when I see the hard sidewalk below merging into the roiling sea. I wouldn't have a chance if I fell. I sit down on the next step to catch my breath and try to slow my heart rate.

The reality is that I can't do this. Chase turns and comes back down to my level. His agile body glides down the steps. There is no fear.

"I can't do this." I gasp.

He smiles and offers me a hand. "You've only just begun, and there are many more steps to climb before we reach the top. Don't look down. Just look at the step in front of you. One step at a time."

I cling to him as he helps me to stand. There isn't room on the steps for both of us to be side by side. He motions for me to go first, indicating that he will be right behind me to catch me if I fall. There's no other way to go. I certainly don't have the nerve to walk back down these steps.

CHAPTER 2

PASAJES TO SAN SEBASTIAN

When I first started thinking about walking the Camino, strange coincidences began to occur. I had gone to Helen's house for tutoring.

"Helen, I don't think I'm ever going to get these dose calculations. They're going to flunk me for sure, and I'll never be a nurse." I groaned, running my fingers through my braids before securing them back with a ponytail band. Lately, playing with my hair had become a nervous habit. A nurse had to score over ninety percent on the dose calculation test—there was no room for error when a patient's medication was on the line. I just HAD to make it through nursing school. Being a nurse was all I had ever wanted.

One of my first childhood memories was of being in the hospital, and I couldn't breathe. My mom was crying, and this nice nurse gave me a special blanket with Hello Kitty™ on it. While she tried to calm my mother down, she said the kitty would watch over me. I wanted to be just like that nurse.

Helen became a main source of encouragement: "Oh Valerie, yes, you will. There are a couple of ways to solve this IV rate problem. Some people get it one way, and some get it another. Let me show you a different way and see if it makes more sense."

"Oh, you are so patient with me. How can I ever thank you?"

"Hey, you helped me memorize all the medications and their side effects. I wasn't sure I could do that," she said.

"OK. Show me again how to solve this problem."

She walked me through the process and said, "Now, solve this next problem. I'll be here to assist you."

I worked it through and looked at her for a reaction.

"Yes, that's it, you've got it now."

"Oh, thank you so much."

"You're welcome. Let's take a break and have some tea."

As I waited for Helen to bring the tea, I wandered from the dining room table into the living room, drawn by a display on her wall. "Helen, are those documents on the wall from the Camino?"

"Yes, that's my credential and my Compostela. Ken had it framed for me when I returned from Spain. When you walk the Camino de Santiago in Spain, you receive absolution from your sins, and they give you a document to prove it."

"You, a sinner?"

"Well, it's a long story," Helen said with a smile.

"Ever since I saw the movie, *I'll Push You*, I can't stop thinking about the Camino," I said, not wanting to pry.

"Yes, the movie is set on the French route, the same one I did with Hannah before she went off to college. It was a mother-daughter trip and so much more. You should do it, not that you are a sinner or anything," said Helen with a wink. "It was an incredible adventure for us."

"I don't know if I can do it. I was born with a hole in my heart. You know, the ventricular septal defect. The doctors fixed it surgically when I was a baby, but sometimes I get short of breath, and it feels like my heart is beating out of my chest."

"I tried to walk too fast at times and got into trouble. If you listen to your body and walk slowly, it shouldn't be a problem. Are you thinking about going after you finish nursing school?" she asked.

"Well, I was thinking about this summer break before our senior year, but Mom still treats me like a baby, and I doubt she'd be willing to let me go."

Ever since Dad died when I was six, combined with my childhood medical problems, she's had a hard time letting me go. She's always been such a helicopter mom. Before that, Dad was always gone running his races. All his medals and photos are like a shrine to him at home. I know she loved him, but she always had to work. She had to take care of me and ensure Dad always had a nice place to rest and train.

When he was alive, I would hear them arguing about finances. Professional runners don't make much money, and he lived to run.

I remember him taking me out on his training runs in the stroller. It felt like flying. All I could see were trees and flowers rushing by. When we were done, he'd lift me out of the stroller and swing me through the air while laughing heartily. He always seemed happiest when he was running.

"Helen, how much did the Camino cost?" I couldn't put the financial burden of such a trip on my Mom. I'd have to pay for it myself. My aid job at the nursing home and living at home with Mom allowed me to save money. I'd have to quit my job to go on the Camino, but I knew they'd take me back. They always need help.

"Well, there are many routes. The plane fare alone is about fifteen hundred dollars. You need to budget about fifty euros a day for room and board. You can make it cheaper by staying in albergues and cooking some of your meals, maybe as low as thirty euros a day," she explained.

I have about five thousand dollars in the bank. "What do you mean by different routes?"

"I walked the French route, the same route in the movie *I'll Push You*. But you can walk from a small town called Sarria to Santiago in about a week. If you choose to go that route, I would plan for a two-week trip, which would include flying time and the bus ride to Sarria."

"Ok, adding up the estimated per day costs and the flight costs equals about twenty-four hundred dollars with the conversion. I can swing that."

"Way to go on the math." Helen laughs. "Whether you go on the Camino or not, that's between you and your mom. But if you go, let me know. I'd be happy to lend you any of my gear and provide any information you need," she offered. "You can wear your running shoes and workout clothes. You don't need anything special."

"That would be great," I said. It's so amazing. I saw the movie, thought about going, and then met someone who had been there. What are the chances?

. . .

Well, the stairs haven't disappeared while I was reminiscing. Helen told me that her pilgrimage gave her the confidence to return to school and re-up her registration as a nurse. She had let it lapse when she got married over twenty-five years ago. She's so smart, caring, fit and strong.

She just whips those manikins around in clinicals. A nurse has to be strong.

Chase looks at me and beckons me to start climbing.

At the top of the stairs, a picnic table is sitting next to a huge propeller. How on earth did they get that up here? I drop my pack on the ground and collapse on the bench. Chase walks to the edge of the lookout.

"You gotta see this."

I slowly make my way towards him, my legs protesting every step. Edging closer to the rim of the cliff, I look out over the blue sea. White plumes of spray are being catapulted into the air as the sea crashes onto the rocks below. I wouldn't like to land on those rocks. I had no idea that heights would freak me out.

"Got your breath?"

"Yes." I'm not even breathing hard. I check my pulse and feel a strong, slow, and steady heartbeat. I'm fine. That was a quick recovery. It must be the running. Back at the bench, I shoulder my pack and see a yellow arrow pointing to my left. I walk down the trail where it joins a road. The arrow points to the right.

"Hey, wait for me," Chase yells, laughing. He points down the road. "By the way, that's how they got the propeller up here."

"What? We could have taken the road."

"Yeah and walked about five more klicks. The shortcut and the view were worth it."

I'm going to have to be more aware. I'm not sure if it was worth it or not.

"Klicks?" I ask.

"Yeah, that's what Europeans call kilometers."

He is so much more worldly than I am. He'll keep me from looking like a tourist.

We make our way through a eucalyptus forest. I love the fragrance of the trees. The air is so fresh and clean. Each breath energizes me.

"Hola," someone from behind us says, and Chase answers. I turn, and there is a woman about our age with dark hair and olive skin overtaking us.

"I'm Emilia," she says in perfect English. We introduce ourselves, and she slows down to match our pace. "Where are you from?"

"I'm a citizen of the world," Chase says, extending his arms as if to embrace the entire earth.

"And I'm from Florida," I say, shaking my head at Chase's exuberance.

"Welcome to Spain. I live in Barcelona, but I love to come here on holiday. Going to San Sebastian?"

"Yes," Chase answers.

"It's the most perfect city in Spain for those who love

the sea and food. Do you have a place to stay?"

"We thought we would stay in the 'muni', La Sirena," Chase says. "We're just going to show up."

"Muni?" I ask.

"Municipal albergue," he explains. "They're run by the Spanish government. We just call them 'muni' for short."

Great. I'm officially the clueless tagalong.

"That should be all right, but I've already made reservations there. It fills up fast with the cheap price and the surfers in town. Do you want me to call and reserve two more beds?"

"Yes," Chase and I say together. Emilia quickly makes the call, speaking in rapid Spanish, and secures our beds.

"So, are you two together?" Emilia asks.

"We met on the airplane, and Chase has been helping me get started," I say, feeling the red heat run up my neck to my face.

"Camino friends are the best friends," Emilia replies and winks at me. "*Vamos.* That's 'let's go' in Spanish."

We head down the road, talking and laughing together, and wind up in a parking lot. There's a yellow arrow on a wooden fence at the far side of the parking lot, pointing towards a dirt path through the trees. The path leads straight down the mountain to more steps that take us to a boardwalk along the sea. Surfers are out in the waves.

Chase was not blowing smoke. This is a surfing paradise. But there's no way I'll be able to join them today. I'm beat.

On our way to the muni, we stop at a grocery store to buy supplies for a fresh fish dinner and breakfast tomorrow. Emilia's been bragging about her cooking skills and the facilities at the albergue, so we're going to see if she can live up to her promises.

Turns out, Emilia wasn't blowing smoke, either. The dinner she made was great. I'm glad we didn't have to wait until eight p.m. for a restaurant to open.

"You look exhausted, Valerie," Chase says. "Why don't you go up to bed? I'll do the dishes."

"I'll help," Emilia chimes in.

Grateful, I make my way up the stairs to our room. We have four bunk beds in the room, but there are just the three of us now. I wonder if anyone else will come in. Emilia and I had already staked out the bottom bunks, and Chase graciously took a top one. He's such a gentleman.

I plug in my phone and connect to the Wi-Fi. Surprise, there's a message from Mom. It's eight in the evening here, so it's two in the afternoon at home. She'll be at work, so I don't have to talk to her. *I'm safe, walked sixteen miles today, no problem. Wish you were here.* The message will satisfy her for a while.

I first told her about wanting to do this after I had gotten home from that study session with Helen.

"How did it go today?" she had asked.

"Great, Helen is so patient, and I finally understand how to solve the dose calculation problems."

"I knew you would. You're so smart. You must have gotten my brains," she said, smiling.

"Mom, when I was at Helen's, she told me that she walked the Camino de Santiago. Remember the movie I told you about that we saw in church? The one about the two guys, one of them in a wheelchair, doing a pilgrimage in Spain. I really want to do it this summer."

"But, Valerie, I don't know if it's advisable with your heart condition, and what about your job?"

"I've already thought about both those things. Helen said I can walk at my own pace, and it would be great to get stronger before I start working as a nurse. Nursing is a very physical job. I could ask my cardiologist and see what she says. I'm sure I could get my job back if I took a leave of absence. They're always hiring nursing assistants."

"Well, let's talk about it after you see the doctor," she replied.

Yep, just as I predicted, Mom put up roadblocks. It was her way of saying "no" but not directly. I knew I'd have to come up with a plan she couldn't object to.

The cardiologist gave the go-ahead, so I asked Helen to meet my mom and help me convince her. Finally, she agreed to let me start in Sarria and walk the final one hundred kilometers to Santiago. This would be a test to see if I could do it, and then maybe I could go back one day and do the whole thing.

When school finally ended for the semester, Helen kept her word and invited me to look at her gear. I couldn't believe she had lived on what was in that tiny pack for over a month.

"Valerie, your pack should weigh no more than fifteen pounds. It's better if it weighs less because you'll add water and snacks in Spain." She had pulled out a small bag containing tape, Vaseline™, and a couple of bandages.

"That's your first aid kit?"

"Yes, and I didn't even use the tape. I used Vaseline™ on my feet every morning before I put on socks to prevent blisters. I did use some of the band-aids on my buddy's blisters. You can buy anything specific you may need at a pharmacy in Spain. Don't take 'just in case' items. They weigh you down. Now if you are on any prescription medicine, take enough in the bottle for the trip with a couple extra pills and the prescription."

I told her I didn't take any prescription medicine.

"Even better." Next, she pulled out a small, red nylon bag

that was zipped shut. She magically pulled a whole jacket out of what became a pocket. "I believe you could wear my jacket, and you may need it in the evenings even though it's summer. Remember, you will be much further north and in the mountains."

That's where it got serious. A few butterflies took flight in my stomach.

"This green bag is the pocket of my poncho," she said, pulling a full-size poncho out of its pocket. The poncho even had a place to cover the pack to keep it dry.

"You only need two sets of clothes, one to wear and one to carry. When you get to the albergue, you wash the clothes you are wearing and put on the clothes you will be walking in the next day. I did take three pairs of undies and socks."

"What about pajamas?"

"If you want to carry them, you can take them, but sleeping in my clothes was fine. Everyone else was doing the same. I got this light nylon string pack at a fundraiser. It was perfect for my shower stuff, clean clothes, and valuables when I went to the shower. Then I would put my dirty clothes in it to take to the laundry. And I used it when shopping for groceries. Most stores want you to bring your own bag. Everything you take should have more than one use."

Next, she showed me her fanny pack and said I could borrow that too.

"And here is my high-tech bag for my Pilgrim's Credential, passport, and credit cards." She laughed as she held up a Ziplock™ bag.

The next thing she pulled out was a gorgeous scarf. It looked so soft that I had to touch it. She smiled and handed it to me. "A good friend of mine had rescued a young woman while walking her Camino. She must have been about nineteen years old. What are you, about twenty?"

"I'm twenty-two," I conceded. "I've had to work some to pay for school, so I am a bit behind."

Helen laughed. "The young woman was working as an au pair in Spain and met my friend, Mary, on her afternoon off. When you are in a foreign country, it is a bit of a relief to find someone who speaks your language."

"I guess I'll have to dust off my high school Spanish. Languages are not my forte."

Helen continued. "The young woman joined them for dinner and, from what I understand, the wine was flowing freely, and she missed her bus back to her job. My friend was not about to let her sit at the bus station all night, so she invited her to stay with them. The next morning, the young woman left to catch her bus and left the scarf behind. Mary gave it to me to take back to the Camino. The scarf was magical."

"Magical?"

"You will have to experience it for yourself." She paused for a moment, then pushed the scarf into my hands. "It's yours. So what else do you need of mine?"

"Are you sure about the scarf? It seems to be really special to you."

"It is special, but it needs to go back to the Camino. It's just hard to let go. It means so much to me."

"Thank you. I'll take really good care of it." I wrapped it around my neck. "Well, I'll borrow the pack, sleeping bag, jacket, fanny pack, and poncho. I have everything else. Is that all right?"

"Of course, I wouldn't have offered if it wasn't. I know you'll take care of my things." We put the gear I decided on into the pack. She helped me into the straps of the pack and adjusted it to fit.

Helen adjusted the scarf and then took a step back. "You look like a pilgrim."

As some of my fears and concerns left me, I felt a little lighter. It was almost like I was taking Helen with me. I removed the pack and unwound the scarf from my neck. I paused and stroked the soft, woven wool. It was so comforting.

Helen looked at me and then at the scarf in my hands. She took it from me and held it close. "You know this scarf helped me get all the way to Santiago. It's also a reminder of a special person I met who gave me the strength to return to nursing school. I hope this scarf gives you the strength to go the whole way. It's not easy. It's a pilgrimage, not a vacation."

I saw her struggle between holding on and letting go. This must be a special scarf.

"It's yours now. You'll know what to do with it when the time is right," she said. "Just listen."

Tears sprang into my eyes.

Helen took a deep breath. "And remember to post pictures on Facebook. I'll ask Hannah to 'friend' you. She can let you know about options that might be of more interest to the younger crowd."

"Helen, are there people on the Camino like me?"

"Oh, honey, many people walk for their health. I saw a man with one leg going along on crutches who put me to shame."

"No, I mean people who are black like me."

Helen paused. "There are people of all colors and cultures on the Camino."

She smiled, and the memories of her experiences flashed over her face. "In some ways, your determination reminds me of a black woman who walked with our group. Emily is a corporate executive, and her Camino intention was to reconnect with her spiritual side. She fulfilled her intention.

That woman is going to set the Catholic church on its ear and become pope one day."

"She sounds wonderful," I said.

"Yes, she is. We keep in touch through Facebook and sometimes by email. Some of the friends you make there, you'll have for life. Honey, you're going to have an incredible experience. You never know what's going to happen and how it will affect your life. Have you set an intention for your Camino?"

"I have been so concerned about getting the clearance to go, I haven't given it much thought."

"Going with an intention is just as important as having the right gear. I suggest you journal and pray about it."

"Just off the top of my head, it would be to know if my body is up to it, if my heart can handle the walking."

Helen laughed. "I know you had a problem with your heart when you were young, but my goodness, girl, you're on a track scholarship. I do believe that you can walk."

"Well, I run short distances, and the coaches are always monitoring us. I will be on my own over there. What if something happens?" I laughed. "Now I sound just like my mom."

"Let's put a couple of apps on your phone." Helen showed me how to download and use WhatsApp. Then she told me about Alert Cops, which we downloaded too. She said I would have to finish setting it up when I got to Spain.

"You call me anytime, day or night, and I'll answer and help you in any way that I can." She straightened the scarf and hugged me. As I left the house, she said, *"Buen Camino."*

CHAPTER 3

SAN SEBASTIAN TO MARKINA-XEMEIN

The sun coming through the window wakes me up. Emilia is still asleep in the other bunk, and Chase is breathing deeply above me. I didn't even hear them come in last night. I tiptoe to the bathroom and do my morning ritual. I can't believe how sore my legs are. I return to the room, and the other two are stirring.

A man in the bunk over Emilia sits up and says, "*Buenos dias.*"

I smile and nod in greeting. Turning back to my pack on the floor, I give him the privacy to get up and start his day. Privacy is definitely relative in community living. I feel the bra and underwear I washed out last night and hung at the end of the bed just like everyone else. They're dry, and I put them in my pack. As I fasten the top of my pack, my doll attached to a loop on the back brushes my hand. I squeeze it and think of my dad, my Abba. I don't remember much about him. He died on a training run, killed by a hit-and-run driver. They never found the driver.

Abba was tall and strong. He would pick me up and swing me around. I remember my braids flying up from my head. It was so much fun. He always did this when he came home from a competition. Mom said he was a great runner and had traveled all over the world competing in marathons. When he came back from a training trip in Kenya, he brought me this wooden doll with the traditional dress. Tears fill my eyes just thinking about this.

Mom says I have long, strong legs just like him. I wonder what he'd think of me doing this. I bet he would support me. He was a dreamer, always pushing himself to get faster and stronger. He never seemed to worry about money. Winning the next race was his goal.

Mom has always been practical, ensuring that the bills were paid, and food was on the table. She would deposit his winnings and sponsorship money into the bank. After he died, this was all that remained of him.

My legs don't feel very strong today. I shake off the soreness and stretch, as I'd seen him do many times. I hope I can make him proud.

Chase and Emilia are moving slowly. I tell them I am going for coffee and offer to bring some back.

"Oh yes, some 'Go Joe' is just what I need. We have another hill to climb to get out of this town," Chase says. They both look about as ragged as I feel.

I return with coffee, and they're all packed up ready to go. We drink our coffee, have toast from leftover bread, then shoulder our packs. The guidebook suggests a twenty-one-kilometer day over a mountain to Zarautz. Shorter than yesterday, thank God.

At about ten klicks, we find a little coffee shop next to an albergue. Dropping our packs on the front porch by a long picnic table, we storm the shop. We are thirsty and hungry pilgrims. I realize that we're disturbing the vibe of peace and quiet, so I immediately quiet everyone down. The lady behind the bar smiles at us and takes our order. The baked goods on the counter call my name.

I go to pay, and the lady points to the donation box next to the cookies. She explains that this coffee shop and the adjoining albergue are part of a community called the "Twelve Tribes." Another woman comes in with refills of coffee cake. She asks if she can join us at the table. We sit, and she explains that they are a Christian sect and follow the teachings of Jesus in the book of Acts. Part of their mission is to provide respite to pilgrims. They grow their food and seek to live in harmony with the earth. She doesn't sound preachy, just informative.

We shoulder our packs and walk downhill toward Zarautz. I wonder what it would be like to live in a community of people. I've heard of hippie communes. Wouldn't Mom just die if I stayed in Spain at a commune?

Chase and Emilia get ahead of me when I slow my pace to make my way downhill carefully. Chase hasn't been quite as attentive today. He must be as tired as I am from yesterday.

When I reach the bottom of the hill, I find them sitting outside a bar, drinking a beer in a little town called Orio. "Is this where we are stopping for the night," I ask.

"No," Chase says. "It's still early. Let's push on. We only have five more klicks to Zarautz, and Emilia has made reservations for us at the albergue. I want to get up early tomorrow and see if I can rent a surfboard and catch a few waves before we start walking. Emilia says the surfing is great and knows just the place."

"Count me in," I say. "Do they rent wetsuits too?"

"Yes," Emilia says. She makes another call and scores us surfboards and wet suits for tomorrow morning.

"You're the best." Chase turns around and smiles at Emilia.

I recognize that smile. He's used it on me too. My heart clenches. "Vamos," I say, echoing Emilia's expression from yesterday, then I wrap the scarf around my neck and shoulder my pack. Chase steps in front of me and adjusts my straps, giving me one of his smiles. My heart melts.

. . .

Six a.m. comes early. We get ready and go to the shop to get our gear. Chase takes a video of the shop and us in our wetsuits, carrying our boards down to the beach. The surf is coming in, gentle rollers all the way from England to the north. They remind me of the waves at Daytona. It's connected to the same ocean, but Florida seems so far away.

I throw my board into the water and then push it into the surf. I gasp as the cold-water seeps into my wetsuit. Once waist-deep, I boost myself up to lay on it and paddle past the break line. The waves are solid curls, 3 to 4 feet high. I line up and watch for the best wave in the set coming in; just at the peak, as the wave starts to break, I maneuver my board into position and feel it pick up momentum. I leap to my feet. It feels solid under me as I drive the board to shore. What a rush! Emilia comes in on the next one. Giving her the thumbs up, she responds, and we paddle out to do it all over again.

Chase is on the beach videoing us with his phone. This is so cool. I know he will share it with me, but I can't post it until I come clean with Mom.

Chase motions for us to come to the beach. "I scored an advertising contract with the surf shop. They'll pay me to post a video about our surfing experience, hoping to draw other pilgrims to take a break and surf here too. I want you two in the video. You're so sexy in those wetsuits. It'll be perfect."

He sets up his tripod, and we have an impromptu chat about the surf and how accommodating the shop is to pilgrims. While Emilia and I clean the boards and rinse out the wetsuits, Chase shows the video to the owner, collects some cash, and posts it on his YouTube channel. I pull up his channel and see he is getting close to the thirty-thousand subscribers mark. No wonder they paid him to post this. I subscribe and go change into my hiking clothes.

We leave the shop and make our way along the coast to Geteria. As we walk into town, I see a café. "This is as far as I am going until I eat." Dropping my pack at an empty table, I pull out a chair and sit. Emilia and Chase follow my example. The waiter comes over, and we order our usual Aquarius.

"Fish and chips," Chase says to the waiter.

"Make that − *dos*," I say.

Emilia dropping her menu on the table, says, "*tres.*"

The waiter takes off to get our food. I notice the tables surrounding us are full of thin, well-dressed young women sipping wine. "I'm a bit underdressed."

Emilia follows my gaze. She smiles and says that she has always wanted to stop here because it's the world's fashion capital, and she wants to visit the fashion museum. The look on Chase's face causes me to choke on my Aquarius.

"Fashion museum. Count me in," I say, winking at Chase. He says he's going to go find a bench to take a nap.

We laugh at the models and some of the fashions, not imagining we would have anywhere to go in some of the clothes on display. Leaving the museum, we realize that it's already four o'clock. Emilia messages Chase, and he replies that we should meet him at the bar where we had lunch.

"This is Carl," Chase points to the man beside him. "He's from Germany."

Carl has sandy brown hair and brown eyes, big enough to drown in. He is taller and lankier than Chase. Emilia and I sit down, and the waiter comes over. "Are we going to walk?" I ask.

"Well, I've gotten out of the notion of walking today," Chase says, "and Carl says there are beds at the local albergue. I vote for more beer and a bed."

Emilia and I agree and order beers.

Chase tells the waiter to add the beers to his tab and then turns to us and says, "You worked today, and I got paid. You earned a beer."

"That's fair," I say.

Helen had mentioned that I might hook up with a Camino familia. I believe it is happening.

. . .

The four of us woke up early today, and we are hitting the trail to Deba. Of course, the first few kilometers are uphill. Then it's downhill to the port of Zumaia. We come to a bridge over a river. I pause in the center of the bridge and drink in the landscape. Looking south up the river into the hills, I can see that the tide is going out, and the colorful small fishing boats bob gently in the current. I post a picture of it on Instagram.

The clanging of the industry and the smell of freshly caught fish make me look north at the port. There are large fishing ships and freighters at the dock. We continue on our way, sharing the bridge and the road with the traffic into town. We stop at a bar and quickly grab some food. The albergue in Deba doesn't take reservations, and we have to get there early to get a bed - four beds, to be exact.

Leaving Zumaia, we climb back up into the hills next to the sea. This is starting to become a pattern. Down to the ports, up the hills to the Camino, then back down to the port. The rivers have carved these natural ports into the landscape. People have taken advantage of the topography emptying into the sea, probably for thousands of years. It's so smart.

The guys are getting ahead of Emilia and me. Their strides are longer. That's alright, she's the one who speaks Spanish.

"Do you have the Alert Cops App?" she asks.

"Yes, my friend helped me download it at home."

"Do you know how it works?"

"Well, actually, I haven't even tested it yet."

"Let me see your phone," she says. She tries to get it to work. "Do you have a Spanish cell phone number?"

"Yes, Chase helped me set up e-SIM."

"Perfect. I'll set up Alert Cops for you even though Spain is very safe, especially compared to what I hear on the news about the US. I believe it is prudent for you to be able to call for help. You may not always be walking with someone who can assist you."

"You're right. I've just been relying on you and Chase to take care of me. I don't think I could call and make reservations like you do or even check the map as Chase does. All I know is following the arrows; and even though I have the app, I just haven't had to rely on it."

"That'll work," she says, and hands back my phone. "Many pilgrims unplug and just follow the arrows. We look after our pilgrims. But I believe in being able to look out for ourselves too."

She's right. I swallow hard, realizing that I have been depending on everyone else to take care of me. What am I doing? I really don't know Chase at all.

We catch up with Chase and Carl, who are drinking beer

at a bar in Itziar. I order an Aquarius. Emilia says to make it two. The guys order refills and a plate of *jamón croquettes*.

"What's that?" I ask.

"They're awesome," Carl says. "They make a dough, add onion and ham, then fry it up into bite-sized pieces. Just what we need to give us the energy to make it into Deba. It's all downhill from here."

When the croquettes arrive, Carl is right—they're delicious. Satisfied, we follow the road downhill. It branches off onto a short, steep path, which empties us onto another road.

Emilia consults her phone. She has notes of each town from friends who have walked this way before. "Start looking for an elevator."

"An elevator?" I ask.

"Yes, many of our towns are built on the side of mountains. We have elevators so the residents don't have to drive or carry groceries up and down steep hills. We can use them too."

"How cool is that?" Chase says.

There's a square building on our left and I realize this is the elevator. We punch the button for the ground floor. It's glass, so we get a bird's eye view of the river below and the village as we ride down. It spits us out into a plaza. After consulting her notes and map, Emilia leads us to the train station. The building looks old, and graffiti is defacing its exterior. We walk around to the south side and up a few stairs. Is there anywhere in Spain that's flat? Just then, a train rumbles into the station. This is not going to be a quiet night.

"Shit," Chase says as he reads the notice on the building, "*Completo*. We're too late to get a bed. Now what?"

"We can try to find a pension," Emilia says. "I know they are a little more expensive, but maybe we can get a room with four beds and a private bathroom."

"Yeah, but that's out of my budget," Chase replies as a couple of well-dressed people walk up to the door, punch the code, and walk in. "I bet tourists are taking up all the space." A snarl appears on his handsome face. It's the first I've seen of a temper from him. "I can't believe they would let tourists sleep in places that are meant for pilgrims."

Carl consults his map. "They probably came here by train. We should walk to the next town. They have an albergue and it's only five more kilometers."

We follow the arrows across a bridge and start up the mountain. Only five kilometers, but of course it's all uphill.

I trudge on. The sky begins to darken as the sun drops behind the mountain. We shouldn't have stopped for drinks and food.

Chase's face looks as dark as the clouds rolling in from the west. We turn onto a dirt path leading into a forest as a few fat raindrops hit us. A clap of thunder has us digging in our packs for our ponchos before we get soaked. Helping each other, we suit up and increase our pace. Then all hell breaks loose. The dirt path quickly becomes a river of mud. I dig my poles in to keep from sliding.

A stream making its way down to the river falls over rocks blocking the path. It looks deep. I don't know how we are going to get across.

"Damn tourist," Chase mumbles, feeding his foul mood.

"Look over there," Emilia says. "A cave. Legends about this area say it is riddled with caves where there are *ermitaños*."

Chase rolls his eyes. "Maybe they'll have us for dinner."

"What are *ermitaños*?" I shiver and wish I had put my jacket on under my poncho.

Chase snaps at me. "Witches. Ridiculous. We can talk later. He steps into the stream that has become a torrent. He slips and falls on his butt in the stream. Chest-deep water rushes by him.

Carl grabs my hiking pole and extends it to Chase who grabs the other end. He jerks hard on the pole to stand up, which throws Carl off balance.

"Not so hard," Carl says. Emilia and I grab Carl and help him pull Chase up and out of the water.

"Now I'm soaked. Whose bright idea was it to keep walking?" Chase glares at Carl.

"Hey, man, I just saved your life."

Chase steps closer to Carl, and his anger escalates with

the storm. The trees rub together when the wind picks up, and they start screeching. Carl does not give him an inch.

"I didn't need your help. You made me look like an idiot."

"Then why did you take it?"

Chase pulls back his arm. I rush between them. He pushes me out of the way. Off balance, we both go down, Chase on top. My backpack prevents me from injuring myself on the rocks.

"See what you made me do." Chase glares at me, grabbing for the scarf around my neck. I shrink back.

"Stop it," Emilia yells. "We have to get to shelter before we get killed."

Carl grabs Chase and pushes him off of me, rolling him back into the stream. He stands guard as Emilia helps me up. "Cool off, man," he says.

"Are you all right?" Emilia asks me. She looks at Chase and mutters under her breath, "*poseído.*"

"I think so," I say as I check myself over.

"Good, then let's check out that cave." She scrambles up the slick boulders on our side of the stream to the entrance of the cave, shining her light inside. "It's empty. Come on up."

I scramble up behind her. She's shaking out her poncho and taking off her pack.

"What did you say? Possessed?" I ask as I take off my gear.

She looks around and moves close to me. "Poseído. It means

an evil spirit inside a person. There is something here I do not like." She walks over to a blackened area at the mouth of the cave. It looks like someone comes here often and builds fires. She takes a chunk of charred wood and draws a large five-pointed star with a circle around its perimeter on the floor of the cave. Then she moves our packs into the center by the fire pit.

"What's that for?" I take the scarf from around my neck, open it up, and wrap it around my shoulders and arms. It is warm and comforting.

"Protection," she says.

"Protection from Chase?"

"I don't know if that's who Chase is or if a spirit from the stream got into him. They can possess us if we are vulnerable. I'm not going to allow myself to be vulnerable."

Well, if it makes her feel better.

"I'm going to check out the rest of the cave," I say. I find my flashlight and look to see how much room there is. The ceiling quickly angles down to the floor, and there is an opening off to the left. My light glints off something at the back of the cave. I crouch down to get there. There's a pile of empty beer cans. I don't think a hermit lives here, but this sure isn't the first time it's been used for shelter.

As I make my way back to the entrance, Emilia watches Carl and Chase come up over the rocks to join us. I suppress a shiver, and I don't think it's because I'm cold. When Chase comes in, I step back and don't take my eyes off him. He approaches, and I keep stepping back. My head bumps into the ceiling. I have nowhere to go.

He offers his hand and says, "I'm so sorry. I don't know what happened. I just lost it."

"Well, no one's hurt, so let's just move on." I walk past him towards the entrance and Emilia's star. I get to my pack, open it up, and retrieve my jacket.

"Looks like this is the party place," Carl says. "There's a supply of wood over here. It must be used regularly by the local teenagers or witches." He motions to the star on the floor. "I'll get a fire going so we can warm up."

Emilia looks at me and puts her finger to her lips.

"Really. Are there witches in Spain?" I ask, because Emilia and Carl are both talking about them like they are real.

Carl winks at me. "I don't believe in witches, but I met one once."

"Let me help," Chase says to Carl, then helps him carry a couple of logs over to the obvious fire pit. Carl rips a few pages out of his guidebook to use as a fire starter. Then he pulls out a lighter and ignites the pile.

"I saw a passageway when I was getting the logs. I'm going to explore," Chase says.

Carl waits until he disappears into the dark, then quietly

says to us, "I don't trust him. We need to take turns staying awake just to make sure we're safe. I'll sit up first." He then raises his voice and says, "Do either of you have any food or water?"

I dig into my pack to see what I have. There's a package of nuts and an apple. I pull those out and put them next to Emilia's two tangerines and chocolate bar. Carl adds a baguette and a hunk of cheese to the smorgasbord. I have two full bottles of water attached to my backpack. I refilled them in the bathroom at our last stop.

"Hey guys, you gotta see this," Chase calls from the passageway.

We grab our flashlights and stoop to make our way single-file down the passageway with Carl in the lead. Soon, he stands up, and we walk into a large cavern. I hear dripping water. There are stalactites and stalagmites littering the space. Three large spirals connected in the center are painted on the wall. They are like a wheel with three curly cue spokes. Between each spiral is a swastika.

"Who do you think left this? Didn't Spain fight on the side of the Germans in World War II?" Chase says.

"The three joined spirals are called a triskele," Emilia explains. "It is an ancient symbol of man, woman, and a universal life force. We believe it was part of the religion of the ancient Celts who came here from Ireland. Different cultures adapted it and have given it their own meaning. The swastika is also an ancient symbol meaning well-being. Hitler stole it and gave it a different meaning."

"Yes, Franco joined Hitler," Carl adds. "My grandfather, who was part of the resistance, told me most of the people in Spain were not happy about joining Germany in the war. You're right, Emilia. The swastika goes back thousands of years to represent well-being. The early Christians used it to signify a long life and prosperity. We have it carved into some of our churches. Hitler corrupted it like he corrupted everything else."

"I didn't know that," I say, moving closer to see if I can determine the material that was used to paint them on the wall. There's some overspray on the edges. "I think someone put these here recently. They look spray-painted. Why would someone do this?"

"There are groups today that keep the old ways alive. Some are Neo-Nazis. They scare me. I know firsthand from my grandfather what the Nazis did. Some are new-age people who are trying to bring back the old ways of peace and harmony. I don't know who came first to this cave, but maybe both groups have used it. The triskele has not been defaced, so maybe it's new-agers or a similar group that promotes universal peace." Carl looks at Chase. "If you hadn't fallen in the stream, we would have never found this place."

"I'm sorry, man," Chase says to Carl. "Well, I don't think any of those groups will be coming here tonight. Let's head back to the fire. This place gives me the creeps."

We follow Chase back to the entrance. When he gets to the pile of food, he reaches for his pack and pulls out a bottle of wine and a bottle opener.

"Now you're talking." Carl picks up the bottle and examines the label. "Nice."

We sit down by the fire, share food and wine, and discuss the symbols. As the adrenaline drains away, sleeping bags are pulled out, and Carl banks the fire. He nods at Emilia and tells her he will wake her up in a few hours.

It is still dark and cold when Emilia shakes me awake to take the last shift. I look over at Chase, and he's asleep.

"Just yell if you need me," she whispers, wrapping herself in her sleeping bag.

I sit and stare at the last few embers, thinking about what happened with Chase. He's been such a gentleman. Then it was like someone flipped a switch, and he turned into a monster. I shudder, remembering how he pulled his fist on Carl. If he had connected, Carl could have been seriously hurt. Carl was just trying to help him. I guess Chase's pride was hurt by falling in the stream, but that can happen to anyone. The rocks were slippery. Maybe he was more exhausted than he thought. It had been a long day, and the beers this afternoon probably didn't help. He did apologize. But I'll be a little more careful around him. I can't abandon him after just one break. He's supported me. I would have never surfed or seen this cave if I hadn't met him. I'll just be a little more cautious.

There's a noise, and I look around. Chase is stirring. He sits up and rubs his eyes. He quietly slips out of his sleeping bag and sits next to me. "You cold?" he whispers.

I shake my head and pull the scarf more securely around my shoulders. He puts his arm around me, and I stiffen. I don't want to wake the others, but I don't want him this close.

I shrug off his arm. He gets the message and hugs his knees. Staring into the embers, he grabs a stick and stirs them. Then he gets up, steps outside to relieve himself, and returns to get another log to build up the fire.

"Is it still raining out there?" I ask.

"No, and I can see a hint of light in the east."

"Good, I'm ready to get out of here."

The flame and whispers wake Carl. He looks at his phone. There's no light. It must be dead. He sits between Chase and me at the fire.

Emilia yawns and stretches. "Buenos dias," she says and starts to roll up her sleeping bag. "Let's go find breakfast."

I pack up my gear. Shouldering my pack, I step to the

entrance of the cave. The sun lights up the boulders we scrambled up last night. Treacherous.

How on earth are we going to climb back down?

Chase seemingly senses my thoughts. "Backward. I'll go first, and you follow. I'll catch you if you fall."

It's like yesterday never happened. He starts down the rocky side of the hill towards the trail, and I slowly follow. Once down, Emilia comes next, and Carl brings up the rear.

The stream is still swollen, rushing down the mountain. The running water reminds me that I have not used the toilet this morning. "Excuse me, I need to step behind a tree."

Emily says, "I'll join you."

As we step just off the trail for privacy, I hear Carl talking to Chase. "See that log over there? I bet we can pick it up and put it across the stream to use as a bridge."

"It's too heavy," Chase says.

"Let's wait for the girls, and we'll roll it," Carl says.

Between the four of us, we position it across the stream. Chase goes first and makes it over just fine. I'm next, using my poles for support on the riverbed. I, too, make it across. Emilia and Carl do the same.

We continue down the path, which turns onto a road marking the entrance to the small town of Olatz. My stomach growls in anticipation of a tortilla and a cafe con leche. The few snacks we had last night did not satisfy my appetite. I have always been a good eater but need the calories to maintain my weight. My friends hate me because I can eat anything and stay slim.

A cafe is on the main street, but the outside tables have chairs stacked on them. It looks deserted. A sign that reads *'Cerrado'* is hanging on the door. We put our noses up to the window to see if anyone is in the bar. All the lights are out, and it's empty. A ghost town. Despondent, we start walking again. We have twenty kilometers to go to the next town.

CHAPTER 4

MARKINA-XEMEIN TO GUERNICA

The slope is slick with mud, dropping steeply downward, and the rain is pouring once more. I cling to saplings with one hand while using my poles with the other, trying to avoid sliding down the treacherous incline.

Are we ever going to reach Markina?

At least we have water. There was a little covered fountain next to the ghost town we passed through. The sign said '*potable*' and I sure hope so. I'm not interested in salmonella, cholera, or some parasite.

As I get to a flatter place in the trail, there is fresh rock and a rope leading down the next steep slope. My hungry stomach is forgotten in the face of this new obstacle. Chase is already hanging on to the rope and slowly lowering himself, hand over hand, down the trail. I skid across the mud to the rope and grab on for dear life. I have no idea how they got the rocks up here, much less to get them to stay so we have some kind of surface on which to place our feet.

Chase takes my hand when I reach the bottom to help me over to the flat dry spot where he's standing. I thank him and remove my hand from his. Emilia comes down next, and Chase helps her over to the flat spot too. He holds on to her hand a little longer than he needs to. Carl follows and easily makes the leap to the dry spot. The dirt path soon ends at a road, and we walk into Markina. The first order of business is food, then a shower and a bed. I don't think I'm even going to wash out my clothes.

We eat a late lunch, then head to the Convento Padres Carmelitas. The convent has forty beds, and we easily fit four together in the same room. The volunteer checking us in holds up his phone to me, and "The worst is over" is written in English next to the Spanish. I am so grateful for translation apps. I can't even imagine how people managed before.

"May I take a picture?" I ask the volunteer and point to the phone.

He gives me a strange look. I pantomime, taking a picture of him and the phone. He smiles and nods his consent.

He uses the translation tool to explain the rules and points to the row of lockers in the common room where we must leave our packs. Each locker has a USB port, which is awesome because it allows us to leave our phones plugged in.

I take a picture of the inside of the locker and of the common room. Then I walk out into the cloister and take another picture. These will make a great post.

. . .

Early the next morning, the common room is quiet as I take my pack out of the locker provided. I tuck the sleeping bag inside, gather toiletries, and quickly stop in the bathroom to perform morning ablutions. Fresh water from the bathroom sink replaces the old water in my bottle. I return to the common room, where the volunteer is making coffee and toast.

My, they work long hours.

I quickly ingest toast and coffee, then make a jelly sandwich, wrap it up in a napkin, and put it in my pack. I'm not going to get caught again without something to eat.

I slip out of the monastery before the rest of the gang gets up. I can do this myself; I don't want to be with them. Carl is okay, but Chase scares me, and Emilia has some weird spiritual practices. I didn't pick them; they picked me. Well, Chase picked me. Lucky me. I need to pick a normal Camino familia if there is such a thing in Spain.

My phone dings.

Damn, is that Chase? Has he figured out that I've ghosted them already?

No, a text from Mom. *Love your post. Glad the worst is over. You must be getting close to Santiago. I hope you are having fun. Call me. XOX*

Mom. Shit. I'm hundreds of miles from Santiago. She expects me home next Sunday.

I find the next arrow, which points me up a rocky path.

Of course, it does. If in doubt, walk uphill.

I charge at the hill, driving my poles into the ground to help pull myself upward. Sweat breaks out.

What was I thinking, following a man to northern Spain? I'm so naïve. He was so kind and excited about the Camino. But what a temper! I don't want to be on the receiving end of that.

I gain elevation, and the mist closes in. Stopping, I drag out my poncho, drape it over my head, and pack. I come to a fork in the path, but there's no yellow arrow. There are no bars on my phone either.

My breath quickens. I have to make a decision. I don't want to walk back down the hill because I might run into Chase. I go left because Emilia said it is always uphill to the next town. The other path goes down. The mist develops into a steady rain, and the dirt path becomes slick under my feet. My throat tightens, and it's harder to breathe.

I throw my pack off to the side of the path and rip the scarf from around my neck. I use it to wipe the rain and sweat from my face. I sit on the ground and lean against a tree, trying to catch my breath. My heart is beating in my ears.

What's wrong with me? Am I having a heart attack?

There are still no bars on my phone. I turn it off and on again, hoping it needs to reboot. Nothing happens. I have to find help. I stand up, using the tree for support, and stuff the scarf into the side pocket of the pack. I shoulder it and start walking.

Mom was right. My heart is not up to this. I'm defective and I'll never be like other people with strong hearts and lungs.

My legs tingle as I try to keep moving. The trees thin, and a field full of sheep off to my left comes into view. There is a gravel farm road running alongside the field. I take the road. There has to be a farmhouse around here. If I can find it, someone will get me help.

I turn left down another gravel road towards the barn in the distance. I glance down, still no bars on my phone. Looking up, I see a house on the other side of the road with smoke coming out of the chimney.

Thank God.

The house looks like it could have been there for centuries. It's made of stone and has a rough-hewn front door painted green. I walk up to the house and knock on the door. An old woman answers.

Oh no, she probably doesn't speak English, and my Spanish is awful. She probably doesn't even know CPR. In my halting Spanish and pantomime, I try to tell her that I'm having a heart attack.

"Do you speak English?" she asks with a kind smile.

"Yes, I think I'm having a heart attack."

"We'd best get you in out of the rain and warm you up with a nice cuppa. Head round the back to the boot room, get out of those wet things, and then come through to the kitchen."

Oh my God. She's crazy too. I'm having a heart attack, and she is offering me tea.

But there's no choice. I walk around to the back of the house and enter a room where there's a place for muddy shoes, boots, and hooks to hang my wet things. I remove my poncho and boots, open the door, and walk in with my pack. I won't leave that out here in the 'boot room.'

She motions me to sit down at the table by the stove. I set my pack beside the hearth of a fireplace so huge I can almost sit inside of it. There's a drying rack that has some clothes on it. Not wanting to mess up Helen's scarf, I pull it out of the side pocket and put it over the rack. The woman hands me a towel and I dry off the best I can. Then I sit in one of the wooden chairs at the plank table. There's a bowl of fruit on the table, which makes me remember that it's been a while since I have eaten.

She asks me how I came to her door. I explain that I'm a pilgrim who has lost my way, and the tears start rolling again.

"How about a nice cuppa and a scone? I've got some fresh clotted cream and jam," she offers.

"Oh, that would be wonderful. I'm so sorry, my name is Valerie."

"Lovely to meet you, Valerie. I'm Fiona, and this is my home. You're very welcome to rest here."

"Where are you from? Your English sounds so... English."

Fiona laughs and tells me she was a Vietnam War bride. She worked at a military base in England when she met a young Spanish Army officer.

"He was so dashing in his uniform, I was smitten the moment I laid eyes on him. Our courtship and marriage happened quickly, as he was being sent to Vietnam. He was stationed in Zaragoza first for training and left for Vietnam six weeks later. When he returned, he was wounded. We decided to come here to his family farm. Family is so important in Spain. Sadly, he never truly recovered from his injuries—some you could see, others you couldn't. He passed away about ten years ago from cancer caused by Agent Orange."

"You didn't go back to England?" I ask as I unzip my jacket. It's getting quite warm in the cozy kitchen.

"No, this became my home, and his family is my family now."

"Where am I?"

"You're on a farm just outside Zenarruza. The town's about a kilometer up the road. You've probably taken a wrong turn down one of the dirt paths—it's easy to do, especially on a day like today. What a lovely scarf! Where did you get it?"

"Thank you. It was given to me by a woman who walked the Camino a couple of years ago. She rescued it and the young woman who owned it. The young woman left it behind, and my friend held onto it. She said it had to return to the Camino, so she gave it to me. I'm very thankful for it, especially today."

"Yes, the weather's very changeable here in the mountains. May I have a look at it?"

"Of course," I say, and I hand it to her.

She takes a close look at the weave and the wool. "Do you know where it was originally purchased? It looks like some of the local handiwork."

"Well, my friend said she was in Estella, on the French way, when she met the young woman who owned it."

"That's not too far," she says.

"Just how far is Estella?"

"Only about 125 kilometers," she says with a laugh. "Yes, walking gives you a whole different perspective. What might take you all day on foot, you can do it in less than an hour by car. My husband and I walked the Camino together when he returned from the war. I believe it helped, but those wounds ran deep. I envy you and your Camino. It was such a special time for us. The nightmares got fewer the more we walked. I reckon it walked most of them right out of him. Och, that was a long time ago. How are you feeling?"

I check my heart rate and breathing. "Much better, thank you. My breathing and my heart feel normal. Is that magic tea?"

"No, but I believe a good cuppa cures many ills. I think you were just knackered and stressed. Sometimes those symptoms can feel like a heart attack, but they're not."

She looks closely at the scarf. "Weaving wool has been part of our culture since the time of the Romans, about a thousand years before Christ was born. Some even believe it was women who invented weaving. It's always been women's work, traditionally. But then, men went and created machines to do it better and faster. I think the woven material lost its magic when the machines took over.

"Women in these mountains still weave in the old way. It's said they infuse their sacred energy into the wool as they wash, comb, dye, and spin it. There's something special about this scarf. See the colors? This combination represents the life force. Women are the givers of life, and anyone who wears this scarf is a recipient of the gift." She smiles and hands me the scarf. "Would you like to see my loom?"

"Oh yes, are you a weaver?"

"I don't have the skill to make something this fine, but I'm learning. It takes years to master. Most of the women here start very young. It's part of the household chores. The women in our town come here, and we spin, weave, and share our secrets."

I knew there was something special about this scarf. How did I end up here?

She takes me through a stone passageway into the weaving room. In the front corner, by the door, is a spinning wheel with a spindle full of yarn. Vats for dying are over by the back door, a loom takes up the middle of the room, and there are a few other things I don't recognize. She explains that the spinning wheel twists the wool into thread. She demonstrates that without twisting, it would easily come apart. She smiles. "Sort of like us humans, we need to be twisted around a bit to be strengthened. Would you like to try?"

"Yes."

She picks up some raw wool sheared from the sheep, cleaned, and carded. I pull the fibers apart, and the smell of dirty socks assaults my nose. Fiona laughs and explains that merino sheep have naturally occurring lanolin – an oil, which is what I'm smelling. She says it's wonderful for the hands and keeps them from chapping in the winter. It's also wonderful for the clothes, keeping them more weatherproof and warmer. She shows me how to pull the fibers into workable bunches and feed them into the bobbin by attaching them to the already spun thread and spinning the wheel.

This is not easy. My yarn is not as uniform as hers. Holding the tension on the wool and pushing those pedals to spin the wheel definitely requires skill. It's work.

Our laughter finishes the tour — laughing at my attempt to weave, that is. I take a picture of her with the loom, and she says I can post it.

We go back into her cozy kitchen. I look out the window into the wet muddy field as the rain continues to pelt down. I know I have to ask how to return to the Camino, but I just can't make myself. Fiona looks at me with understanding and asks if I would like to stay for dinner and the night. With a huge sigh of relief, I accept. It's not a hard sell.

She busies herself about the kitchen and asks me to help with chopping vegetables for the soup. She puts broth on the stove and sears the meat and onions in a cast iron skillet so they will retain their flavor. She then adds the vegetables to the boiling broth and puts the lid on the pot so it will simmer.

She takes me up a small staircase to the guest room, takes a towel and washcloth out of the cupboard, and leaves me to clean up. The room has the basics and is warm and cozy. The quilt on the bed looks like it could have been there for a hundred years. There's a small wooden chest of drawers and hooks to hang my clothes on.

The bathroom is utilitarian, but the water is hot. After bathing and dressing, I walk downstairs with my travel-stained clothes and ask where I can wash them. She points out a sink in the spinning room and motions to the drying rack by the fireplace, which holds Helen's scarf.

I finish my laundry, and she hands me two brightly painted ceramic bowls to set on the table. She then sends me to the cellar to get a pitcher of wine, butter, and cheese. She unwraps a loaf of bread from a cloth and asks me to slice it. She says she had baked it the day before. The yeasty aroma is tantalizing. I'm starving.

We sit down to eat. She bows her head and asks for grace and blessings on the meal and for me. Tears well up. She pats my hand and fills my bowl with the savory soup. When we finish the meal, she tells me to leave the dishes, then tops off our wine. Taking a sip of wine, she leans back in her chair and says, "Tell me, how did you come to be on the Camino, knocking at my door?"

I begin to tell her all about my friend Helen, the scarf, and the hole in my heart. And how Helen had walked the five hundred miles of the French Way when she was forty-two years old and how I knew I had to try.

Then I tell her about meeting Chase, what happened at the stream, and how I left the albergue early to escape from him. Then the rain came, and I got lost.

I let her know that my mom doesn't know I am in northern Spain. She thinks I'm almost to Santiago. "I just don't know what she will say if I tell her the truth. I just have to go home."

"Oh, my love," Fiona says. "I'm so sorry. You're not the first pilgrim to stop here and rest, and you're certainly not the first to find yourself on a different road than you planned. I do think you need to tell your mum the truth. I've got Wi-Fi. You can give her a call."

"You're right. I can't keep this from her any longer. I'll call her tonight when she gets off work."

"She'll be cross that you lied to her, but she'll forgive you. Then in the morning, I'll take you back to the Camino. We're about five kilometers from the crossroads where you missed the turn."

"Thank you." I sigh.

"The Camino is a pilgrimage, it's tough, and it's not a competition. I walked it again after my husband passed, hoping it would heal the pain in my heart. I still miss him. I learned that I simply had to keep on living. By carrying on and moving forward, I'm honoring all that he gave me."

"Oh, Fiona, I so want to honor myself, to find the strength within me. I have to be strong."

"Strength isn't all it's cracked up to be. Rocks will break and transform. They become the pliable earth that sustains our existence. It's resilience, my dear, that will see you through. Just get up and walk. See where it takes you."

"Is that all I have to do?"

"Yes, just put one foot in front of the other and keep after it day after day, and you'll not only reach Santiago but also discover what an amazing young woman you are. Now, get some sleep, and I'll take you back to the Camino in the morning to set you on the right path."

"Oh, thank you so much." I hug her, and she hugs me back.

I go up to my room and take out my phone. Sucking in a deep breath, I call Mom.

"Hi, how are you?" I ask.

"Wonderful, and you?"

She sounds wonderful. In fact, I haven't heard her sound this happy in a while.

"I'm good." I pause. I hate to spoil her mood.

"That didn't sound very good."

"Well, I have a confession. I'm in northern Spain, walking the Norte. I won't be home next week. I'm going to stay longer."

"What? Can you afford that? What made you change your mind?"

"I met a person on the plane, and he convinced me to change my plans." I sound so lame.

"And who is this person?"

"He's a pilgrim like me and a gentleman. We're walking with a bunch of people about my age. It's safe." I don't want her to worry. "And tonight, I'm staying with a lovely lady in her house. We fixed a great meal, and she gave me a soft bed to sleep in. It's raining, and I'm so glad to be in where it's warm and safe."

"Slow down, Valerie. You're in northern Spain with a group of young people staying at a lady's house?"

"Yes, it's not at all like home. There are people who welcome and take care of pilgrims. This woman even weaves and told me all about the history of the scarf. It's so cool."

There is silence on the other end of the phone.

"I'm sorry, Mom, I know this is a surprise, and I haven't been honest with you. Fiona, who owns this house, encouraged me to call and she is right."

"Well, I'm glad someone has some common sense. So how far are you from Santiago?"

"Well, if I finish the Norte...and I want to, it's so beautiful... I will be in Santiago in about...a month?"

"A month?"

"Yes, I have worked out the money, and we're staying in really cheap places and cooking a lot of our own meals. It's fine." I feel so bad for screwing up her good mood.

"Please check in with me often so I know you are all right. And I'm going to call Helen and talk to her."

"Helen had nothing to do with this. She thinks I'm close to Santiago like you."

"At least she knows about Spain. Did you change your flight?'

"Yes, ma'am."

"Well, just keep me informed."

"I will. And sorry for bringing your mood down."

"I'm still wonderful and worried. I knew that one day I was going to have to set you free, but I didn't think it would be this soon."

"I love you, Mom."

"I love you too," she says.

I let out my breath, not realizing that I had been holding it.

. . .

I wake up and look out the window. The fields are glistening as the first rays of the sun catch the remnants of last night's rain, creating a soft, sparkling glow. Fiona serves me a delicious breakfast, and we then get into her car.

She takes me back to the Camino and points to an arrow leading down an asphalt road. She hugs me, tightens the scarf around my neck, and says, "Buen Camino."

I have no words.

The birds are singing their morning song as I walk along the road in the clean crisp air. There's not another person in sight. My legs and feet feel strong as I make my way up the mountain toward Guernica.

CHAPTER 5

GUERNICA TO CASTRO-URDIALES

So far, they haven't caught up with me, or maybe they passed me when I was with Fiona. Either way, I'm fine.

I am fine. My heart's behaving, my legs are strong. Fiona gave me food for snacks and some extra if I got caught out. The yellow arrows appear just as they should. I can do this.

I don't need Chase to guide me. Though I do miss him. A warm sensation flows through my body, and it's not the walking that's doing it. Maybe he was just having a bad day. I mean, the rain and getting caught out in the dark would put anyone in a bad mood. Maybe I ghosted him too soon.

I take a break at the next arrow. It points to a dirt path that goes straight uphill. A horse wanders over to the fence where I am standing, looking for a handout.

"Sorry, girl." I look underneath her. She's a mare, and she looks pregnant.

We were told not to feed the animals, and I understand why. I don't know if they are on a special diet or taking medicine, and I wouldn't want to hurt her or her baby. I rub her nose and walk on.

Maybe Chase is worried about me because I didn't even say goodbye. But he hasn't even tried to text me. Maybe he hooked up with Emilia. Well, I don't care. There really wasn't anything between us anyway. And maybe he came into my life just to get me to take the more challenging route. Maybe it's the Camino magic that Helen talks about, giving you what you need, not what you want.

I hear the city of Guernica in the distance. It's amazing how much noise a city makes. The path ends at a highway, and I'm suddenly waiting at stop lights and looking both ways before I cross the street.

Following the arrows, I stop in front of a huge tile mural—Picasso's Guernica. Even I know the Picasso style. The strange cubism stands in stark contrast to the ancient buildings that have been bombarding me since I arrived in Spain.

Another pilgrim walks up beside me. At least I assume she's a pilgrim. She has a backpack and dirty boots. Her grey hair is tucked under her hat and there are laugh lines beside her eyes. She reminds me of what Helen must have looked like on her Camino.

"Fascinating, isn't it?" she says. "Not one of our better times in history."

"What does it mean?"

"It is a reminder of the horrors of war. This city was almost destroyed by bombs. Just down there is the Peace Museum, and up there are the bomb shelters. American?"

"Yes, my name's Valerie."

"I'm Gretchen. Are you staying here tonight?"

"Yeah, I guess. But I'm not sure where to go."

"You're in luck. I'm staying at the youth hostel, and they have beds."

I sigh in relief, and follow Gretchen back the way I came to the hostel and pay my eighteen euros, which is not cheap. Inside the dorm, I find a bunk, put the paper sheet I had been issued on top of the vinyl mattress, and then put the paper case on my pillow. Gretchen comes over and asks me to join her for dinner. My stomach rumbles in response, even after devouring some of the food Fiona gave me.

We find a small cafe and order wine and tapas.

"Where did you start walking?" she asks.

"Irún, and you?"

"Same. Are you going to Santiago?"

"I don't know."

"A true pilgrim, walking where the road takes you. I'm on a short holiday. I will finish my Camino in Bilbao.

Just two more days. I'll come back and walk another week next year."

"Where are you from?" I ask.

"I live in Italy, but I'm an expat from Chicago."

"An expat?"

"Yes, that means I'm from America, but I'm now a citizen of Italy. I have dual citizenship."

"You can do that?"

"Immigration doesn't just go one way. I love Italy, and it's much cheaper for me to retire there than in the U.S.," she explains.

It's amazing that a person can become a citizen of another country. I never thought of it that way, but it does make sense.

"I'm a retired archeologist and love the ancient cities. It's wonderful to live close enough to frequent them and volunteer on digs."

"So cool." I pick up a round piece of bread with chopped tomato and put it into my mouth. The flavor explodes.

"Good, eh?"

"Delicious." I reach for an olive, pop it into my mouth, and wash it down with wine. "Archaeology—it sounds fascinating."

"It is. I believe that we must have a firm foundation, an understanding of our past to build our future."

"Hmm....I can see that." Maybe that's why I feel a pull to understand where I came from.

"Are you walking alone?"

"Well, that's a long story. I came to Spain alone, then I met a man and ended up here on the Norte instead of on the Frances."

She raises her eyebrows at me.

"I ghosted him."

She pats my hand. "Do you want to walk with me tomorrow?"

"Yes," flies out of my mouth before I can stop it.

I've been fooling myself. I really don't know where I am or what I am doing. I'm so lucky to have bumped into her at the mural.

We return to the hostel, and Gretchen pulls out her paperback guidebook. It's seventeen kilometers to Larrabetzu, where there's a donativo. She makes the call and secures two beds.

"What's a 'donativo'?

"Oh my, you are a new pilgrim. It is an albergue like this, but there is no set charge. You pay what you are comfortable paying."

"How do they survive?" I ask.

"Most pilgrims are grateful and pay their way. It's what some call a 'grace economy.' That means people share the wealth. You may need a bed, and they may need someone to clean, cook, or provide groceries or cash. There is an element of gratitude in living this way. And speaking of groceries, I saw a store on the way here. We'll stop and pick up food on our way out of town tomorrow."

An economy of grace. I love this.

. . .

Yesterday we walked up the dirt paths through the forest to Larrabetzu. We had such a lovely night, and I put ten euros in the donation basket. Then we headed to Bilbao, where Gretchen had secured us two bunks at the Poshtel, close to the Guggenheim Museum.

Today, we are going sightseeing. We start with breakfast at a cafe and then take the pedestrian bridge to the old town and the Cathedral de Santiago. A statue catches my eye, so I walk up to get a closer look.

"This cathedral was built in the fourteenth century," Gretchen says as she comes up beside me. "You're fascinated by the Black Madonna?"

"Yes. Do you know anything about her?"

"Well, not this one in particular. But Black Madonnas date back to Medieval times. There are about four to five hundred in the world, most of them are in Europe. Several theories have been offered as to why they were constructed this way.

"Some say that was the only material available to the artist and so they used it. Some say that the Madonna must be a woman of color because she was from the Middle East. Some argue that they were repurposed pagan statues when the Catholics sought to erase all pagan art. They were just re-carved and dressed up to look like a Madonna. Others argue that it was done intentionally to symbolize biblical and cultural references to fertility, motherhood, and the earth. Some have African features along with the color." She looks closely at me.

I feel myself squirming under her microscopic gaze.

"I mean no offense," she says as she turns back to scrutinize the Madonna. "Not really African, but maybe a combination of races."

"Sort of like me. My mom is of mixed race, going way back to slave times. She is lighter skinned and has more European features than my father, who was born in Kenya."

"Yes, there are very few pure races anymore. And I, for one, believe this is a good thing. We are all on this earth together and need to support and love each other. I believe this is what she stands for. Sort of like the many colors of your scarf. It adds a richness and vibrancy to the world."

I smile at her. I love this interpretation.

We get a stamp and then make our way back across the river to the Guggenheim. After being immersed in ancient art and architecture, entering a museum of modern art is a shock. I love how Europeans preserve their past while making room for the new.

We go back to our hostel, and Gretchen takes a shower while I lay on my bunk, going through all the pictures I have taken today. It's so amazing. I pick out my favorites and post them on Facebook and Instagram. It's a relief not to worry about posting something that may give my position away. Now Mom can see that I really am all right.

Checking Chase's Instagram, I see he is ahead of me with Emilia in Portugalete. There's no mention of Carl. Gretchen is leaving to go home, and I'll be alone again.

· · ·

After breakfast, we stand at the front of the hostel waiting for Gretchen's taxi. She hands me her guidebook.

"I know having a paperback book is old-fashioned, but I find it easier and more informative than the apps. I won't need this again. I'll get the new one next year."

Tears jump into my eyes, and I don't know what to say.

She pats me on the hand, smiles, and says, "You have this. You'll be just fine."

She grabs her pack and gets into a taxi to the airport. I shoulder mine and look for the next arrow as I make my way towards Portugalete. I wonder if Chase and Emilia will still be there when I arrive. I doubt it. Do I really want to meet up with them? Look what's happened to me since I have walked alone. I've met two wonderful women who took care of me. Helen told me that the Camino provides, and so far, it has. I stroke the scarf around my neck, finding comfort in it.

The arrows point me down the main roads flanked by stores, apartments, and industry. If I wanted an urban walk, I would've stayed home. Clouds roll in and I pull my poncho out of my pack and cover up. It doesn't take long for the rain to start in earnest. The puddles get deeper with every step, and a bus goes by, hits a puddle, and sprays water all over me even though I'm on the sidewalk.

Why on earth did I let a man make plans for me? I find myself clenching my teeth. If Mom could see me, she would say, "Don't let anger ruin your teeth." Well, who cares about my teeth anyway? There's a puddle ahead, and I stomp right through it, soaking my shoes and socks. Who cares? They're my feet. I'm going to jump into every puddle I see.

The arrow points left up a hill. Of course it does. The road leads out of town into a forest. I put my head down and lean into the mountain. I walk out of the rain as I top the hill, then I take the mud path down back into the mist. A root grabs the toe of my shoe, and I immediately extend my poles to stop the fall. They slip out of my wet hands, and I fall on my butt, legs straight out in front of me. It's a slide, bumping over roots and rocks. I reach for them to slow my descent. Finally, I grab a passing sapling and stop myself.

"Are you all right?" A man calls down to me from the top of the hill.

I check for any broken bones. There are none that I can tell. Just my butt hurts. But it's big enough to cushion me. I look up, and he is slowly making his way from tree to tree down the hill.

"I'm all right. Just my pride." I pull myself up.

He hands me my poles. "I noticed you left the rubber tips on. You may want to take them off when you are on muddy paths. They'll give you more traction. Are you going all the way to Portugalete today?"

"I think so." I blink back the tears as I remove tips like Chase taught me when I bought them. I put the tips in the baggie in my pack pocket. We continue to walk carefully down the hill. My wet pants are uncomfortable against my skin. My rescuer's gray hair peeks out from under his hood, and his tan face shows the lines of a life spent outdoors. His hiking pants are stuffed into the top of his boots. His rain jacket comes down past his hips. His accent tells me he is Spanish, but he speaks English well.

"I have walked the Camino three times. The French route when I left the service, the Ingles with my buddy from England, and this route with my wife a few years ago. This is the most difficult of the three. You are a brave young woman taking this on. Are you walking alone?"

"Well...uh..no," I quickly add. "My friends are just ahead. I'm slower downhill than they are. If you hadn't come along, I would have yelled for them." I don't want this strange man to think I'm all alone out here. I don't know what he would do to me. If he starts anything, I'll scream.

"Well, I'm glad you have some friends out here. But Spain is very safe for young women. I'll walk with you until we meet up with your friends. I just want to make sure you don't have any unseen injuries that may surface as the adrenaline gets out of your system."

"Oh, you don't have to slow down for me. I'm fine." He looks all right and has been very kind, but I'm alone out here, and there isn't a town for six more kilometers.

"I had just retired from the Guardia Civil. I met so many pilgrims patrolling this stretch of the Camino that I had to walk it myself. My wife wouldn't hear of me going alone and joined me. She is tougher than I am," he says as he winks. "We live in Barakaldo. I walk up here to keep fit and to watch after pilgrims."

"I'm so grateful for you being here to help me." I sure hope he's telling the truth. There is a ring on the fourth finger of his left hand.

As we walk, he tells me about the eucalyptus forests. He says that these used to be hardwood forests, but eucalyptus trees were planted when the wood was harvested. They grow fast and can be harvested quickly. Because it's an oily tree, it burns fast, and now there are problems with forest fires. But the people who own the trees make good money, and they employ many people. Northern Spain doesn't have a lot of industry, and this keeps us from losing some of our young people to the cities.

"I've seen a lot of changes in my seventy years on this earth," he says.

"Seventy? No way. I thought you were much younger."

"Why, thank you, young lady. It must be the hiking and good clean air."

"Yes, the air is much cleaner than where I live in Florida."

"I hear Florida is really hot. You all have set record temperatures."

"It is hot. And we have forest fires too."

"Yes, climate change is negatively affecting the entire world. I'm sorry. My name is Jose."

"I'm Valerie."

"Valerie, a nice name. What does it mean?"

"It means strength and health. Apparently, I had a very loud, strong cry when I was born, and my dad named me."

"I bet he's proud of you for taking on this Camino."

"Oh, he died when I was six."

"I'm so sorry. He was young. He watches over you."

"Why do you say that?"

"You took a bad fall but did not get hurt. I was put in the right place to help you. Our ancestors help us in the same way we help them by remembering. The tree that stopped your fall is an oak. They're not as plentiful anymore. The oak is the tree of life and the legends surrounding it date back to Druid times. Armegin, the great Galician Druid, obtained his knowledge and strength from the oak."

"I didn't know that. I do know the oak has been used in the past for medical purposes and the acorn for food."

"Yes." He nods and encourages me to go on.

"Sometimes I feel like my father is with me. I brought a piece of him with me in the form of that doll on the back of my pack. When I was sliding down the hill, I felt like I would be fine. I know that sounds strange."

"No, it doesn't. You are very connected to your ancestors. Here in Spain, we have very strong roots in many belief systems. We have been through so much. There is one constant, and that is taking comfort in the cycle of life and nature. Our woods are full of those who are tricksters and those who protect us. The tricksters teach us lessons, and our protectors keep the lessons from being too harsh."

"I thought everyone was Catholic here. But I did meet a girl who believes in possession, and she's with the guy I came here with."

"He left you?"

"Well, it was more like me leaving him. He started acting strange, and I got afraid of his temper."

"Smart girl. So they are not just ahead?"

That was dumb. My stomach starts flipping, and my heart starts beating a little faster. I just let him know I'm alone. "Well, they are ahead, but I'm not sure how far."

He smiles. What can a seventy-year-old man do to me anyway? And if he were going to hurt me, he would have already. We've not seen another person.

At the top of the next hill, we start back down, but this time on a forest road. We walk in silence. I take the guidebook out of my fanny pack and look for a place to stay in town. I have to get cleaned up.

"Why don't you come to our house? It's on the edge of town. My wife will fuss over you and get you clean. And she'll feed both of us," he says as if reading my mind.

Should I trust him? He seems harmless enough, and he's married. I don't get a creepy feeling about him.

I try to protest, but he suggests that I wait until I meet his wife before I make a decision. This makes sense. If I'm uncomfortable, I can just keep walking.

. . .

I get up early. Jose's wife, Lucia, fixes me breakfast and a sandwich for the road. She is so kind. They both are. I shouldn't have worried. She has already done my laundry and dried it overnight by the hearth.

Jose helps me settle my pack on my back. Lucia retrieves my scarf from the drying rack, carefully folds it lengthwise, and winds it around my neck. It's warm from the fire. She pulls me into an embrace, kissing me on each cheek. I walk out the front door, turn and smile. They are waving goodbye. So cute. Turning back, I see the next yellow arrow is at the corner.

What a wonderful couple! One of their children and two of their grandchildren joined us for dinner last night. It made me wish for a big family. Mom's parents live in New York, so I don't get to see them often. Dad's family lives in Kenya. I've never met them, but I would love to visit them sometime.

I'm not going to catch up with Chase and Emilia anytime soon. They're probably two days ahead of me now. I'm ok.

Actually, I'm better than ok. I went up and down those hills yesterday and didn't get lost. I've met amazing people and have clean clothes. Gratitude. I am a pilgrim.

I wonder what Jose meant about my being connected to my ancestors. I never told Mom, but there are times when I talk to Dad even though he is gone. I had a dream one night of being with him and his parents as a child. It felt like I was really there with them, not just in my dream. But I never told anyone. I didn't want them to think I was crazy.

The forests give way to the sea, and I'm once again walking on top of the cliffs. The rhythm of the Camino becomes part of me as the kilometers disappear under my feet. Every now and then, a small group of pilgrims walk by, call out 'Buen Camino' and keep going. I jump off the path to let a peloton of bikers pass. I would be scared riding a bike along the edge of this cliff, but it doesn't seem to slow them down at all.

I really thought Carl, Chase, and Emilia would be my Camino familia. Though I believe it would have been a dysfunctional familia, I shake my head and laugh at myself. First, I want people around and then I don't. I don't know what I want.

CHAPTER 6

CASTRO-URDIALES TO GÜEMES

I can smell the sea as I make my way down the mountain to the outskirts of Castro-Urdiales. The residential section gives way to a boardwalk along the beach. I stop at a grocery and buy a bocadillo, fruit, and an Aquarius. Taking my picnic with me, I find a bench overlooking the tidal basin with sailboats swinging from their moorings.

It reminds me of going to the small village of Gulfport and watching the boats in the basin. Mom and I would often go there for the market and craft shows. However, this town is much more ancient.

There's a fortress and a church on top of a hill on the peninsula, which sticks out on the other side of the basin. I wish Mom were here to share this. I envy Helen walking with her daughter. It must have been wonderful.

"Is there room for two?"

I look up and Carl is smiling at me. I move over to share the bench. "I thought you were ahead with Chase and Emilia."

"Emilia went home in Bilboa, and I've no idea where Chase is. And you ghosted us. Can't say that I blame you based on how Chase acted."

"I never thanked you for standing up for me."

"A man should never hit a woman. You did nothing wrong. I'd do it again."

"I was scared. I just couldn't stay with you all, and I took off."

"Smart girl." He pulls a bocadillo out of his pack. "Nice place for lunch."

"Yes, I was just thinking about a small town back home with a boat basin similar to this one."

"How about after lunch we go out and tour the church on the peninsula? There's an old fort and lighthouse behind it."

"That sounds perfect. But I need to check into the muni first and ensure I get a bed."

"Good idea." Carl nods and smiles.

We throw our garbage in the trash, make our way to the muni, and secure our bunks for the night. After dropping our packs on the floor by our bunks, we walk out to be tourists. It's amazing how I can walk in the evening after walking all day, though it's much easier without the pack.

Carl leads me through the old part of town, up old stone steps. On the landing, there's a sign pointing west for the Camino, and I tuck this away in my brain for tomorrow. We continue up the stairs to the church. Carl tells me that the Gothic church, with its flying buttresses, dates to Templar times. He points out all the carvings in the main entrance. I'm surprised to see rabbits, oxen, and dragons instead of the more traditional Catholic symbols. He explains that the symbols represent abundance and protection.

A volunteer offers to stamp our credentials, and we give a donation to the church. Then we make our way behind the church to the lighthouse, whose foundation and fortress walls also date back to the Templars. Carl says that the Templars were tasked with protecting the Camino and its pilgrims. He tells me they were the ones who originally set up the credential system for getting stamps. They would hold onto a pilgrim's money then use it to pay their bills. The stamps are a record of proof that the pilgrim had stayed or eaten at that inn. It's the predecessor to the credit card.

I've been so busy just surviving that I'm missing the history and culture of this country. I stand at the edge of the old wall and look out into the sea, where small sailboats zip around a course in the fresh breeze. I can imagine this was a busy fishing port that needed the protection of the fort and the church.

We make our way back down the steps to the old town. Cafes line the square, and the smell of food reminds me that it's been a while since lunch. We find an open table and sit down. I peruse the menu. A few familiar words jump out at me. I order pescado, ensalada y vino tinto.

"Well done," Carl says after he puts in his order. "This will be the freshest fish and salad you have ever eaten. The fish was probably brought in today by boat, and all the vegetables are locally sourced. How did you and Chase meet?"

I guess he has a right to know the story since he did rescue me. "I met Chase on the flight to Spain, and he convinced me to change my plan and walk the Norte with him instead of walking from Sarria to Santiago."

"Wow, he must be very persuasive."

"Yes, he is. And it was working out well until that day out of Deba. Then all hell broke loose. I would have never guessed he had that side. It was a tough day, and he did take a fall. He must have been embarrassed."

"Anyone can fall, and being embarrassed is no excuse to go after a lady."

"Well, I'd like to talk to him again and get an understanding of what happened. But I need to get some space first. He was very kind and fun to be with until then."

"Good riddance, I say." Carl picks up his fork and knife when the waiter puts the plates in front of us and tucks into his meal.

The fish flakes off the bone, and the fried batter is so light. I let the delicate flavors melt in my mouth. The salad is crisp and fresh, just as Chase said.

"Well, if you do hook up with him again, make sure it's in a public place." Carl lifts his wine glass to me. I lift mine and clink his glass in agreement.

. . .

We get coffee, bread, and jam for breakfast at the albergue and make our way back to the stone steps. We follow a stone sidewalk between the sea and the street. The sea has carved out natural pools of water in the rocks. I have to look twice at the realistic statues of children diving off the rocks into the turquoise pools. There are no swimmers today. The fresh breeze of last night has turned into a cold wind. I am grateful for Helen's puff jacket, and I pull the scarf further up my chin.

"I'm walking to Liendo today," Carl says and points to a grocery.

"Good idea." If I can buy groceries most of the time, stay in albergues, and eat out only occasionally, I should have enough money to make it to Santiago. At least, that's what I told Mom. She has enough financial worries without me burdening her.

I ask Carl if he wants company. He nods, and I try to imagine his story. He seems to be old and wise, yet he's also youthful. Wrinkles don't mark his face, and his brown hair has the highlights of someone who is used to being outside.

"How did you get enough time off to walk the Norte?" I inquire, trying to start a deeper conversation.

"I finished University in May and wanted to do the Camino before I find a job as an engineer."

"What kind of engineering?"

"Construction. I like to build things. That's why I enjoy exploring these ancient ruins. The builders of the past were incredible engineers with such limited tools. The church and walls we walked on yesterday have been standing against the elements for nearly a thousand years."

"You must have studied history also."

"It was more like engineering history, how the great cathedrals and fortifications were built. I enjoy seeing what I studied. It adds another dimension. Why are you walking the Camino?"

"I just want to test myself and see if I can. And I want to become stronger for my career as a nurse." The words sound so lame.

"Sometimes we walk for one reason, and something totally else happens," he says as if he'd read my mind.

"That I totally agree with."

We walk on in comfortable silence. The Camino turns inland along a river. We cross over the river and start climbing another mountain. I can't keep up with Carl's stride and level of fitness. I stop to catch my breath and take in the horses and cows grazing along the farm track. I walk until I start breathing hard again, then stop and relax.

Carl is just ahead, sitting at the summit. He pats a spot beside him on the ground and rummages through his backpack. He pulls out a tangerine and hands it to me. I break it open, and a spray of citrus bursts into the air. The fragrance makes my mouth water. It's so sweet that I quickly devour it. I place the rind back into the plastic bag that Carl holds out for me. We stand up and make our way downhill to the next town.

We spend the night in Liendo at the Saturnino Candido albergue. It's only eight euros.

· · ·

The next morning we grab a coffee and a tortilla at a local café as we walk towards Laredo. Carl decides to stop at the Church of Santa Maria de Asunción and gives me a tour of this ancient but still active church, which was built in the thirteenth century and has five naves. We then walk down the ancient stone road towards the beach. Stopping at a grocery store, we grab a bocadillo for lunch, and I buy extra fruit to share.

The town thins out, and the way becomes a boardwalk beside the sea, stretching as far as I can see. There are a few people out running for exercise. As the sky starts to darken, the cold wind is keeping the tourists away. A sign for a yacht club and restaurant is just ahead. There's an old, abandoned pier and warehouse between them. We walk along a sandy path between the restaurant and the warehouse that dumps us out onto a desolate dead-end beach. The beach juts out into a pass between the river and the sea. There are no signs or yellow arrows.

I consult the guidebook, and Carl looks at his app. The book says we must catch a ferry out of Loredo to go to Sontono, or we will be stuck walking the long way around to get to a bridge to cross the river. The map shows the ferry coming in where we are standing. When the rain starts to fall, we pull rain gear out of our packs and walk back towards the cafe. Deciding to divide and conquer, Carl goes to the yacht club, and I go to the cafe.

I don't want to retrace any steps. It's hard enough walking the Way without having to retrace mistakes. My mood plummets with the rain. There are some other pilgrims coming across the parking lot, along with what could be townspeople. I stop them and ask about the ferry. They point me back towards the empty beach. A boat is making its way toward the end of the beach, where it juts out into the pass. It takes me a minute to realize that this is the ferry and it's going to pull up to the beach. I text Carl and take off running towards the yacht club, my pack bouncing against my back.

Carl emerges from the club, his hands and shoulders lifting in the classic "I don't know' gesture. I signal for him to come with me. He quickens his pace as I point towards the beach behind the restaurant. I walk back to the beach, with him closely following behind.

He reaches me as the ferry drops a gangplank onto the beach. We look at each other in amazement. With Carl at my heels, the first mate puts his hand out to steady me as I walk up the steep, slick gangplank into the ferry. The other passengers move closer to each other under the small, covered sitting area.

Carl chooses to stand out in the rain. The first mate pulls up the gangplank and collects three euros from each of us as the ferry crosses the inlet. Any chop on the water is being beaten down by the rain. The ferry glides across the river in no time and pulls up to a dock in Sontoro in what looks like the middle of town. There is an arrow pointing right, but Carl shows me that his GPS is showing us to go left through the town for about two kilometers to the albergue.

We make our way to the youth hostel across another bridge on the outskirts of town. The rain is not giving us a break. The hostel is part of a recreation complex with sailing dinghies in the yard, a gym for team sports, and racquetball courts. A young woman checks us in, men in one room and women in another. She provides the obligatory paper sheets and pillowcases. I stake out my bunk and head to the shower.

The shower reminds me of gym showers in high school. It is a large, open room full of shower heads and a drain in the middle. Women of all ages and shapes are doing their best to maintain a bubble of privacy. I follow suit. At least the water is hot.

I meet up with Carl in the common area, and we make our way to the dining room. It reminds me of a school cafeteria. Really? Am I back in high school? The chairs are on the utilitarian Formica™ tables, and there's a stainless-steel caldron with a spout for water and coffee. Empty. A couple of women have commandeered a table and are heating food in the microwave. A sign reminding us to clean up after ourselves hangs above the microwave.

The guidebook indicated that the albergue offered a community dinner. Wrong again. I'm ready to trash this book. There's no food or open restaurants close by. We pull a couple of chairs off a table and get some paper towels from a holder on the wall. I share my remaining orange with Carl.

He pulls out an old pack of nuts, apologizing that this is all he has left. We eat in silence.

There is nothing to do but go to bed and look for food in the morning. I crawl into my bunk in the quiet of the dorm. Sounds from the gym below filter up to us. Someone down there cranks the music, and it sounds like a party with balls bouncing off the wall. I put in my earplugs, wrap the scarf around my ears, and toss and turn.

I finally give up and go down to the gym. A man at the door refuses my admittance. He indicates this is a private event. I turn around and climb the two flights of stairs back to my dorm.

. . .

The sun's streaming in the window and the other women in the room are rising and packing. I take care of my morning ablutions, grab my pack, and meet Carl by the front door. We retrace our steps back over the bridge. At the next intersection, we find two yellow arrows, one pointing toward the commercial docks and the other arrow pointing back into town. We consult the app to see which way to go. On the opposite corner from us, there is a small cafe full of dock workers in for coffee and breakfast. We head for food instead.

Now done with breakfast, we choose the path through town. On the outskirts of town, I can tell we are close to the sea from the salt smell in the breeze. The path turns north, then turns left by a prison. A prison with a water view. This would be prime real estate in Florida and not wasted on a prison. The old walls must be at least twelve feet high with new razor wire on the top. I wonder if recreation time includes a dip in the sea.

We pass the prison and walk through a small town. At a side street we see an arrow pointing down a sandy track towards the beach. There's a wooden split rail fence with a gap leading out to the beach and an arrow pointing west along the edge of the fence towards a hill with trees and rocks. We follow the poorly marked path to the hill and see that it winds through trees and boulders up a cliff.

Carl looks at me, nods, and takes off up the path. Reluctantly, I follow. The path becomes steeper, and the trees and bushes close in. I cannot see past the next hairpin turn through the undergrowth.

The path turns into mud where rivulets of water flow from the rain last night. I stop at one of the turns to breathe and can just glimpse the sea below through the trees. I've lost sight of Carl. Going back down is not an option. I check my poles and remove the tips. Well, at least I'm doing something right. I look for a place to anchor my poles. I am not going to slide down another hill on my butt. I take each of my next steps carefully, bracing myself on roots and rocks in hopes they don't give way.

I make the next turn and begin heading downhill. There's no summit or view at the top, and the path down is even more treacherous. Carl is probably down by now, and I don't care. I'm going to proceed at my own pace. I don't want to start sliding out here all by myself. I stroke the scarf, and it comforts me.

The path dumps me out onto a beach. Carl is in the distance turning off the beach towards a town. I catch up with him at the only small cafe in sight, and we have a silent meal.

We consult our guidebooks. We've walked eight kilometers to the town of Noja. Then it's fifteen more kilometers to Güemes, a donativo albergue. Everyone says it is a must-stay place. The arrows point us through the middle of town as we turn inland. Passing a grocery store, we duck in to purchase some snacks. I don't want to be caught without food again.

CHAPTER 7

GÜEMES TO SANTANDER

It's back into the mountains. The sun is shining, and I start to sweat. My legs dig in as I ascend the next rise. The donativo albergue at Güemes operates on a first-come, first-served basis, so I push myself to keep pace with Carl. The terrain consists of farmland interspersed with forest, and we mainly walk on roads. The footing is secure, and we can make good time.

A large hacienda comes into view on a hill surrounded by pastures and a copse of hardwoods. Of course, we have to walk up the final hill to the hacienda. A volunteer meets us by an arbor. He indicates that we must remove our shoes and put them against a fence with our packs. We sit in line on a bench in the shade, and he serves homemade cookies and water from a spring on the property.

A man somewhere behind me yells, "Valerie!"

Chase comes around the corner. He runs over, lifts me off the bench, and swings me around. "I've been so worried about you. I didn't know where you went. You haven't responded to any of my texts."

"I didn't get any texts from you."

"Well, I did text you that day in Markina."

"Oh, yeah, I didn't have service and then got caught out in the rain. And besides, I wasn't sure I wanted to walk with you anymore."

He gets a hurt look in his eyes. My heart melts a little.

"Why not?"

"Well, what happened after Deba scared me, and I just took off."

"I thought you were tougher than that." He steps into my space and grabs my upper arm. "You let a little night of rain in a cave scare you."

Carl comes to stand beside me. Chase lets go and steps back. There's a storm building in Chase's blue eyes, and his smile becomes a thin line.

The lady checking everyone in calls out, "Chase, please show this couple to their room." She points to an older couple who I bet have been married for years; they look and dress alike.

"Sure," he says, then turns to me. "I'll see you later."

Carl and I exchange glances. My stomach clenches. I pull

out the guidebook. There's no other place nearby where we can stay. At least there are a lot of pilgrims here, so I won't be alone with Chase.

Two cookies and two cups of water later, it's finally our turn to check-in. We provide our credentials and passports and are told we will be shown to our rooms, which are segregated by gender. We are also told to attend a mandatory seven p.m. lecture about the facility before the community dinner.

Chase comes back with two sets of paper bedding and shows us to our separate rooms. I snag a bottom bunk with an outlet in the women's dorm. We had walked by a washing machine, so Carl and I agreed to meet to do laundry after we shower. It'll be nice to have fresh, laundered clothes instead of half-clean ones from a sink. There is even a dryer, so we don't have to use a clothesline. What a luxury!

I meet Carl in the laundry area and start the machine. He goes to take a nap. I wander around the extensive grounds and find a round building with beautiful murals on the walls. Its ceiling is made of wooden beams in a spoke pattern to match the room's round shape. There are benches around the edge and a stack of pillows if one wants to sit silently on the floor.

The room is empty and inviting. I sit on a cushioned bench and lean against the wall. My eyes are drawn to a skylight above me. The glass is fashioned in the same spoke pattern as the ceiling. Every detail is beautiful and well thought out. I touch the scarf around my neck where it crosses over my heart. A feeling of peace envelops me as I rest my hand over my heart.

Closing my eyes, I can smell the residual smoke and candle wax from a previous meeting. The cool air in the darkened room comforts me. By the grace of God, I have made it safely this far. I focus on breathing in through my nose and out through my mouth, allowing my diaphragm to expand as I breathe in and contract as I release all the tension with my exhale. My mind empties, and I drift into a feeling of bliss. Chase's voice jolts me back to the room.

"There you are," he says, now standing in front of me. "Oh, you're meditating. I'm sorry for disturbing you. I was just so excited to see you sitting here alone. We need to talk." He sits beside me.

"You did disturb me, and I was meditating. I thought this was a sacred space."

Oh God, that was snarky. I hope I don't piss him off. There are people nearby in case he does something foolish. I can scream.

"It is. And it's the perfect place for us to talk. What happened to you? We got up that morning in Markina, and you were gone."

I grip the scarf tightly. "I needed time alone, like now."

"I really have missed you, and you never answered my text. I thought maybe you went home."

"No, I met some other pilgrims and walked with them and sometimes on my own," I say, trying to indicate that I really don't need him.

"You mean you hooked up with Carl. I saw how he was staking his claim on you out front."

My blood starts to boil. I stand up. My bliss is gone. Turning my back on him, I walk out of the room. I don't want my anger to disturb the peaceful vibes in this room. He catches up with me on the grassy lawn at the back of the albergue near the fence by a corral containing cows.

Pilgrims are sitting in small groups on towels on the lawn, soaking up the late afternoon sun. We are out of earshot but within view of the other pilgrims. Chase puts his arms around my waist from behind. My body goes stiff. I can't believe his audacity.

I grab his arm and turn, untangling from his grasp. "Don't touch me." I look him straight in the eye.

"Oh Valerie, are you still sore about me slipping and falling with you in the stream? I apologized. It was an accident."

"You scared me." I glance over his shoulder at the pilgrims on the lawn. Their presence gives me courage, and I know I can get help if I need it.

"It was such a downer day. You were so angry for no reason. I was afraid you would hurt someone or hurt yourself. I tried to stop you from hitting Carl, and we both tumbled," he explains.

"What?" I suck in and release a huge breath. "You were the one going after Carl."

"Oh, you must have really been exhausted. That's not how it happened. I was surprised to see you here with Carl after how he treated you."

I shake my head to clear my mind. "That's not how I remember it going down," I say. I brush past him and head back toward the albergue. He grabs the end of the scarf, which jerks my head. I yank the scarf out of his hand and run towards a group of pilgrims sitting in a circle on the lawn.

Suddenly, Carl is at my side. "I saw what was happening from the balcony. I'm sorry it took me so long to get down here."

Chase approaches us. "Now I see how it is. You're dumping me for him." He points his finger into Carl's face.

"No, Chase, that's not how it is. We've just been walking together, and there's nothing between us." I grab his finger and hold on tight. I don't want a scene or Carl to get hurt. I tell Carl, "It's all right, I can handle this."

"You heard the lady," Chase says as I release his finger. "Go. We need to talk some things out."

Carl looks questionably at me. I nod and take a seat on the grass. Carl walks away, and Chase sits next to me.

"I'm sorry," he says. "I shouldn't have lost my temper. You have no idea how much I've missed you, and you show up with him."

"I know what it may look like to you, but it's not what it seems. Carl is a nice man, but there is nothing between us that way. Besides, he has a girl back home." I lie about "the girl back home" to placate him. We have to make it through this evening without bloodshed. Carl could have a girl back home, and she would be very blessed. He's a good man.

"Are you working here?" I say, changing the subject.

"Yes. Father Ernesto, the man who owns this place, needed some help with some projects and the pilgrims. He's giving me room and board for free as long as I work. Volunteers do everything you see here."

"It's beautiful." I breathe again. The crisis is averted, but not over.

"Yes, we're turning the stables over there into private rooms for pilgrims. Do you want to go see it?" He sounds so proud of his work, like a child needing reassurance.

"All right." The timer buzzes on my phone. "But first, I have to go put the laundry in the dryer, and I really need to rest. We walked over twenty-four kilometers today. Why don't I meet you at the stables at about six-thirty p.m., before the seven p.m. mandatory lecture? What's that about anyway?"

"Father Ernesto or one of the volunteers tells everyone about the history and mission of this community."

"Cool. I'll see you in about an hour." I walk to the laundry room. Carl is already moving the clothes from the washer to the dryer.

"Are you sure you're all right?" he says.

"Yes, he just wanted to apologize for his behavior," I say, which is mostly the truth. I pull a couple of euros out of my fanny pack to feed the dryer. "Thanks for taking care of the laundry. I'm going up to my room for a nap, but I'll set my timer."

"Ok, I'll see you back here when it's dry. There is a long line of people waiting for the dryer."

I make my way to my room. There are six bunk beds, all staked out with blankets or sleeping bags. The woman across from me is looking at her phone. I lay down on my bunk and plug in my phone.

There's a friend request on Facebook from someone named Dot. I check out her profile. She looks like a sweet old lady, so I confirm our friendship and give her a wave. Then I post a couple of pictures of the albergue and let everyone know where I am.

The lady on the bunk across from me says, "Hi, my name

is Ana. I saw you with Chase. It looked like sparks were flying. He's hot."

"My name's Valerie, and the heat you saw needs to have a bucket of ice water thrown on it."

"So you two aren't an item?"

"No, we are not."

"So he's fair game."

"Knock yourself out." I turn my back to her and close my eyes.

. . .

The alarm goes off and I get out of bed. Walking downstairs, I realize that the soreness I experience every day when I first stand up has disappeared. I must really be getting into shape.

Carl and I separate the laundry. I take mine to my room and throw it on my bed, to be put away later. I really don't want to be late for my meeting with Chase. We need to get this, whatever it is, back on an even keel.

Chase is standing by a building that looks like it used to be a stable. The white walls are so clean and fresh. He shows me where they have transformed each stall into a room with four bunks and a bathroom. He says that he's learning about plumbing the bathrooms from one of the permanent volunteers. No one here works for money. It is a community of people sharing the chores. They use materials discarded by the locals in town and create these beautiful buildings and works of art. Even the permanent volunteers aren't paid. Their needs are handled through donations collected from the pilgrims. Any extra money is sent to third-world countries to assist the poor.

Sharing the work and reaping the rewards from the work is such a different way to live. No money – just receiving what you need, not what you want.

There's a hint of pride in his voice, and I ask, "Are you planning on staying here a while?"

"I don't know. It feels right now. Why don't you stay a couple of days? One of the girls is leaving tomorrow, and we could use the help in the kitchen."

"I don't know. You already derailed me once." I laugh.

Chase laughs as well, his blue eyes sparkling. "I'm so sorry, Valerie. I hurt you. I don't know what got into me. Spending time walking alone and now staying here makes me take stock of myself. I thought I had grown beyond my temper, but then it jumped out in jealous rage when I saw you with Carl."

"There's no need to be jealous of Carl."

"I know that now. And I know how much more work I need to do to find a place of peace in my soul."

I touch his arm, and he pulls me into a hug. He lets go when a bell rings. "Time to go to the meeting." He gestures toward the sound with his head.

Saved by the bell. But it does feel good to be back on even ground. I hate that he was feeling so hurt. But isn't that why we walk the Camino? To face our demons and learn about ourselves?

We make our way into the meeting room. Ana and Carl are sitting together and motion for us to join them. After an entertaining lecture about the origins of the albergue and Father Ernesto, the four of us walk to the dining room. Chase excuses himself to go serve dinner.

"Well, that's a huge turnaround," Carl says.

"Turnaround?" I ask.

"Yes. Chase seems so mellow and kind all of a sudden. Maybe he just put on the sheep's clothes to keep us guessing?"

Stroking the scarf, I say, "Maybe people can change."

"It sure didn't look like that this afternoon," Carl says.

"I was tired and cranky and gave him what for. He was just reacting to it. We have it worked out now."

"So maybe he's not available," Ana chimes in.

"Slow down. I didn't say I was ready to marry the guy. I just don't want to write him off as a friend. We're all out here facing our demons, and sometimes it goes sideways."

"How charitable of you," Carl says, his words thick with sarcasm.

Chase brings out a tureen of soup and sets it on our table. He returns with a basket of bread, sets it right in front of me, and smiles. A peace offering. Warmth seeps through my body.

Carl turns to Ana and asks where she's from. Their conversation fades from my awareness as I reflect upon my relationship with Chase. In the beginning, he was so charming and supportive. I felt safe. Then there was that one huge break of anger, and I can tell he's still embarrassed by it. We are all a work in progress.

. . .

It's breakfast, and Chase delivers the toast to the table. "So, are you going to stay a couple of days?"

"No, I have decided to continue walking. I didn't intend to be in Spain this long. I have to make it all the way to Santiago before my money runs out."

"I understand. Would you like some company?"

"I thought you were here for a while volunteering."

"That's the beauty of this place. Volunteers come and go. Someone had just left when I arrived, so I decided to stay a few days. Seeing you reminds me that I, too, must continue on my journey. I can't hide out here."

"Well, you're welcome to join us," I tell him, indicating Carl and Ana.

"Great, I'll let Father Ernesto know. I will meet you out front with my pack after breakfast clean-up."

Chase hurries away and Carl gives me a hard look. "Really? You invited him to walk with us without asking first."

"You don't have to join us." I flip my braids over my shoulder and rearrange the scarf around my neck. "You can walk your own Camino."

"Sounds good to me." Carl doesn't seem so happy with the way this is going.

I look at Ana. "I'm going to walk with Chase. You're welcome to join us or walk with Carl—whatever you want to do."

"I'll hang with Carl for a while."

The butterflies in my stomach, quiet for the last couple of weeks, begin to resemble a dog fight. I push the rest of my toast away and make a stop at the donation box. I drop money in it to cover my night and meals. As I start to walk out the door, Father Ernesto catches my eye and beckons to me.

He extends both of his hands, and I take them. As he looks deep into my eyes, I feel like he is touching my soul.

"Follow your heart, and peace will be with you." He hugs me and then smiles.

I return the smile with tears in my eyes.

Back in my room, I brush my teeth, grab my pack, and breathe deeply before I meet Chase.

CHAPTER 8

SANTANDER TO UNQUERA/BUSTIO

The road takes us north through the coastal mountain range and back to the sea. The scent of the salt on the breeze from the Cantabrian Sea reminds me of home. The rich smell of the farmland and the acrid smell of the livestock remind me that I am still a long way from my home on the Gulf of Mexico.

The road becomes a dirt path as we turn beside a corral with a goat peeking over the wooden rail fencing. I wave, and he bleats at me. I bleat back, and we have a little conversation over the fence. Chase laughs at us. I love his laugh. He grabs my hand and pulls me away from my cloven-hooved admirer toward the sea.

The path snakes its way along the edge of the cliff. I will never get tired of these views. I wish Florida were not so built up along its shore. The view of the sea is so relaxing, everyone deserves to be able to enjoy it. The Spanish got it right.

The fresh breeze keeps us cool as the sun beats down. I'm so grateful for it. And I'm grateful to be sharing this with Chase. I squeeze his hand, and he smiles at me. We come to a stile, and being the perfect gentleman, he helps me over it. I believe his outbursts were part of his journey. He seems contrite about the two incidents. The second flare of temper at Güemes was not as bad as the first one. Helen alluded to the fact that the quiet time on the Camino assists you in learning about yourself.

I've learned that my heart is a lot stronger than I thought. Climbing is so much easier now, and even my initial fear of heights has faded as I relish the beauty.

The path starts to descend towards a beach. There is a parking lot with camper vans, and there are surfers on the sea below.

"How did the surfing post work out?" I ask Chase.

"It went viral. I give credit to my two models. You all looked so hot out there surfing, and the afterglow in the beach interview was just insane. The shop is really pleased. They would like me to do some more work for them."

"I'm so happy for you. So are you going to take the job?"

He doesn't answer and we continue our descent to a sandy overlook. The details of the surfers are much clearer, and the regular curling waves make me want to join them.

"We are in negotiations right now," he finally says. "But I'm getting footage just in case. In fact, stand right there. I want to get some footage of you looking out at the surfers. There's such longing in your eyes." He points his phone at me, catches my profile, and starts the video.

I turn and look into the lens. "You're right. I would be out there in a hot minute if I had a board and a wetsuit. The sea is calling, and I must obey." I laugh and turn back to the sea.

"Wow, Valerie. That was sick. You slayed it. Your talent is going to be wasted as a nurse. You're a natural in front of the camera. Just imagine what we could do."

"Chase, really. This is fun, but it's not my jam. This whole experience seems like a dream. In a few weeks, it's back to reality."

"Reality is what you make it."

I start across the parking lot full of surfer vans and try to imagine myself living that lifestyle. Dad loved to travel to races. Traveling was part of his life. He would come home and fill me with stories of the things he saw and did. I could feel Mom's disquiet. She got lonely when he was gone, and she worried about his safety and finances all the time. I wonder if she's afraid that I'm following in his footsteps.

I wonder if my taking off on this pilgrimage throws her right back into the space of worrying about him and his finances when he was traveling.

"No," I say. "I need a secure job, not to run off on a whim. I won't let Mom hold the bag on this one. She has paid her dues."

"What is security? People get laid off, or they don't get paid what they're worth. Are you going to go hide in a hospital for the rest of your life? Cleaning up the mess of others instead of living your dreams. YOLO. You only live once."

"My dream is to become a nurse. I don't see it as cleaning up messes. I see it as helping people heal."

"Well, when you are old and grey and still taking out bedpans, let me know if it was worth it."

I'm not going to rise to the bait.

"I'm going to be that rich nurse who is needed around the world to use my spectacular healing skills while you are languishing under a bridge." I laugh and start up the path to the top of the next cliff. He catches up and grabs my hand.

From the cliff's top, I can see the water boiling when it hits the rocks below. My stomach clutches, and I deliberately slow my breath. It would be awful to be thrown off this cliff into the sea. I reach for the scarf with my other hand and hold it tight. I'm not in any danger. I'm so dramatic.

Turning west, the city of Loredo is spread out before me along another stretch of beach. I release Chase's hand when we reach a steep descent where the path winds down to the beach. The arrows disappear when we reach the beach. We follow along the sand between the water and the sea oats. The pilgrims in front of us have dropped their backpacks on the sand and removed their socks and shoes to relieve their sore feet in the salt water. Chase and I follow suit. The cold water is so refreshing.

Now barefoot, we stuff our socks in the toe of our shoes and tie them to our packs. With our packs shouldered, we walk through the sand to where the boardwalk starts. There's a cafe right on the beach. We don't say a word and drop our packs at a table. I go in to use the bathroom. There's a smorgasbord of food laid out along the bar. My stomach rumbles.

After using the bathroom, I stop at the bar to get something to eat. I go back out to our table after I pay my bill. Chase already has his lunch and has invited a couple of young female pilgrims to join us. They are talking and laughing at his entertaining pantomime. The universal language.

After we eat, we head through the town toward the harbor. The girls join us. We must catch a ferry across the Bay of Santander to the city. The bay is huge, reminding me a bit of the Port of Tampa. Freighters and cruise ships come in and out of the channel in an orderly procession.

At least this ferry has a dock and is larger than the last. We disembark on the other side.

"Are we going to stay here tonight?" I ask.

"No, too expensive," Chase says. "Let's get out of the crowd and keep going. There's a small town just eight more klicks ahead. We will all stay at the albergue."

The two girls, Isabel and Jade, agree. "Santander es muy caro. Santa Cruz es mucho más batata."

"I like cheaper," I say as we follow the yellow arrows through the city. There's a park along the waterfront with life-size statues where we pause and take pictures. Then we leave the waterfront and head inland towards the cathedral, stopping to get our credentials stamped. The girls pause to kneel in front of the altar. I join them while Chase watches from the back of the church.

As we leave the city behind, the road sharply rises. I feel disappointed. I would have liked to see the Palacio de Magdalena. The guidebook said that the sea lions come up to the sun on the rocks by the pools.

Once again, we are thrust into the roller coaster of mountains as we head back inland.

Please, God, let there be a place for us to stay. I don't want a repeat of the last time we left a perfectly good city behind.

Taking matters into my own hands, I pantomime to our companions, trying to ask if there is room at the albergue in Santa Cruz for all of us. Isabel pulls out a phone and calls. She reserves four beds and gives me the thumbs up. There is an advantage to walking with Spaniards. Thank God.

The sun is shining, and all is good in the world. Hugging the scarf, I send Helen thanks through the ether for encouraging me to embark upon this journey and keeping me safe.

. . .

We have gotten up early to head to Santillana del Mar. Jade searches the name of the town and hands me her phone. It reads, 'Don't let the name fool you.' There is an old saying that Santillana del Mar is the town of three lies since it is neither a Saint (*Santo*) nor flat (*llana*), nor is it by the sea (*Mar*) as implied by its name.

However, the name actually derives from Santa Juliana (or Santa Illana), whose remains are kept in the Colegiata, a Romanesque church and former Benedictine monastery.

I stop at the wall of the city and look up at the crenellations. "OMG, look at this town."

If I were an attacking force, I would think twice about entering this village. The cobblestone streets are artfully laid out and uneven under my feet. Pennants are flying from rooftops, and a banner is hanging down the side of the castle wall. A long line of people is waiting to go in.

A stone church is just ahead. We walk into the plaza and follow the arrows around back to get our credentials stamped. Outside the church office, we wind our way through town. Small shops line the pedestrian street with local wares, food, and souvenirs. It reminds me a bit of Key West.

"You all know they use this town as a backdrop to films set in medieval times," Chase says, using the camera on his phone to film the ambiance of the place. "I bet I can get a few customers here. What do you think, Valerie, another chance for a starring role in one of my infomercials? It will be perfect." He pulls a headpiece with rhinestones off a display and puts it on my head. "You look like a princess."

The Spanish girls stroll on ahead and disappear into a shop with cheeses and sausages on display. Chase points his camera at me and takes a picture, then turns on the video and asks me to say a few things.

Tongue-tied, I remove the headpiece and replace it on the display stand.

"I thought you were all in with me."

"I am, but you caught me unaware. I'm not an actress."

Chase goes into the shop and asks to meet the owner.

While he is wheeling and dealing, I wander across the street. They have some beautiful dresses on display, fit for a princess. I don't think I'd like to wear a corset and be imprisoned in my clothes, but they sure are pretty. I can see where the tight bodice would make even my small décolletage show some cleavage.

Chase comes up behind me and encircles my waist with his arms. Leaning down, he whispers into my ear. "I'm so sorry I put you on the spot. You're such a natural. I forget that you have so little experience." He looks at the dresses on the rack in front of me and stops at a crimson one with lace around the bodice. He gently pushes me to the side and takes the dress off the rack. "Now, this one would just set off your ebony skin. Women would flock to buy one."

The proprietor asks if I want to try it on.

"Go ahead," says Chase. "I'll wait here."

I change in their fitting room. As I walk out, I adjust the neckline to show off my new look. The proprietor pulls a silver headband with ruby stones off a rack and puts it on my head.

Chase has his camera ready. "You don't have to say a thing. Just walk up and down the street. Pictures say much more than words."

I feel so self-conscious, but when I start to walk, the Spanish girls come out of the sausage and cheese shop.

They sway their hips and grin, giving me the thumbs up. I sway my hips, and the dress sways with me. It's so sensual. Spinning, I feel the fabric lift and swirl with me. A small crowd gathers, and I laugh uncomfortably. My face must be as red as the dress. A man in a medieval costume comes by, takes my hand, and leads me in a few dance steps, then bows. I curtsey in return. He heads down the street.

Chase puts his phone down, lifts me, and twirls me around. "You are really something special."

We head back into the shop where I change and leave him talking to the owner. As I come out of the fitting room, money exchanges hands. Chase shakes hands with him.

"So, did you make your fortune?" I ask.

"Well, enough to pay for the albergue and dinner tonight. Let's head on to the convent," Chase says. "We need to check in and get a room."

We follow a maze of winding streets, with stone walls blocking our view. The cobblestone street leads to a main road with a parking lot for tourist buses and a sign points to the convent across the street.

Chase, the girls, and I are assigned a cell in the convent with two sets of bunk beds. Chase opts for the top bunk, and I take the bottom. The Spanish girls take the other bunks. We shower, and the girls and I wash clothes while

Chase edits today's video. We hang our clothes on lines in the garden and relax in the sun until it's time for the community dinner. It's simple fare but delicious. I love this minimal lifestyle. Maybe Chase is onto something.

Dinner is now finished, so we go back out into the garden. The clothes have dried. I fold them and take them to a table where Chase and the girls are enjoying a bottle of wine that Jade had purchased in town. The evening light intensifies the color of the flowers, and Chase takes advantage of it, asking the Spanish girls and me to pose. It's much easier with a couple of glasses of wine in me.

The girls gather their laundry and head up to the room. Chase and I stand in the garden, watching the last of the sun's rays disappear over the stone wall. He puts his arms around my waist and pulls me close. I turn my face up to him for a kiss. At first, it is gentle, and then, as desire and fire take over, it's like he is devouring me.

"Get a room," a male pilgrim calls out to us. Chase flips him the bird and laughs.

I step back out of his grasp. This is a little too intense for the situation. But oh my, if we were in private, I don't think I would want to stop at just a kiss. My whole body wanted to respond.

. . .

The next morning we rise early and follow the yellow arrows out of town. The contrast of this medieval city to the surrounding countryside of trailers and dirt paths is stark. The Spanish girls have decided to walk with us. I'm relieved. I don't think I'm ready to take my relationship with Chase to the next level. But thinking about that kiss creates an ache in my loins. I don't trust myself with him.

The route becomes a series of hills, blocking our view of the sea. We make our way through the countryside to Comillas on the coast. We follow the road down a hill to the river, which dumps into the sea. It is still a couple of kilometers to the beach from town, so we head to our albergue instead. The girls have reserved us a room.

This town, like the route to get here, is all hills. We shower and do laundry, and we're heading down the narrow streets to find El Capricho de Gaudi. Gaudi designed this home for a rich businessman named Máximo Díaz de Quijano. We stop at the booth to pay the entrance fee. Chase balks at spending the money, so I offer to buy his ticket as a gift.

We walk into the front garden. The house is whimsical in typical Gaudi style and has a tower on one side decorated in a checkerboard pattern with green tiles and sunflower tiles soaring above our heads. The stone pathway leads behind the house to a terraced garden. We are to meet our tour guide in the garden.

We wander into a hidden alcove in between the rocks and hedges, and Chase grabs me and kisses me. "Thank you. What a beautiful gift."

The guide calls for us to gather at the entrance to the house, where we join our group. The house is amazing. Máximo was also a musician, and musical motifs are everywhere.

We walk through an arboretum. I stop to look at the plants and statues. The place is so tropical, and the plants remind me of home. It's like Gaudi brought the outside in.

I tell Chase, "I definitely want one of these in my future home, filled with medicinal plants."

He blanches, then quickly covers it up with a smile. "That sounds nice," he says. He gives my hand a squeeze and pulls me into the next room to join the tour.

We end the tour in the music room, where there is a display of photos of the house, Máximo, and Gaudi. According to the dates, the house was completed in 1885. Máximo moved in on June 30th and died on July 7, 1885, one week after he moved in.

OMG. I turn to the tour guide, pointing to the dates.

"Yes, the dates are correct," he says. "Máximo never got to enjoy his home. He was ill when he moved in and never recovered."

"How sad," I say.

Chase puts his arm around my shoulders, "Like I say, YOLO. Enjoy it while you can."

Each lost in our own thoughts, we leave the house and walk down the hill to the main square. There's a supermarket to buy groceries for dinner and snacks for the road tomorrow. We trudge back up the hill on the other side of town and go to our albergue. The Spanish girls take over the cooking, Chase pours us wine, and I post on social media.

. . .

Under a sunny sky, we leave town via a sidewalk beside a busy road. We quickly get back out in the countryside and follow a path down towards a beach and river to the town of Oyambre, through the national park of the same name. A dirt road then takes us away from the sea, over the hills, and back to the sea to the next port town of San Vicente de la Barquera.

I see a grocery store, and we go grab lunch and snacks. The asphalt road quickly turns onto a farm track. Chase suddenly stops, and the Spanish girls keep walking. I stop and turn back towards him. He motions to the dirt track, but I don't see anything.

"My shadow," he explains and points again.

I stand beside him, and my shadow expands to meet his. He takes a picture with his phone.

"This is so iconic. Every pilgrim has a picture of their shadow. We are so tall. We can do anything we want and reach any height. I am the king, and you are my princess."

He takes my hand and kisses it. Laughing, I curtsey. We then go back to the business of walking.

Shadows. I always understood my shadow side to be the part of me that is hidden, even from myself. The part of me that can trip me up if I let it. Chase sees it as his power. Hmm...

"*Cuidado, sal del medio*," Isabel calls out.

As directed, I look behind me. A herd of cows is running down the hill toward us, followed by farmers in cars and trucks. I jump to the side of the road beside the Spanish girls, and we get as close as possible to the barbed wire fence.

"Let's run with the cows." Chase laughs, ignoring the call for caution, and starts to run alongside a bull with horns. The bull swerves to miss him and causes the other cows to swerve towards a barbed wire fence on the other side of the road.

"Stop," I yell at Chase.

"Come on, it's fun," he yells back.

There's no way I'm going to join him. The mooing increases and the farmers let their dogs loose from the cars. The dogs start to turn the cows back into the road, away from the barbed wire. The farmers yell at us in Spanish, and the girls turn white. I look at them for a translation.

Jade shows me her phone. "'Crazy pilgrim, you hurt our cows.'" She gives me a look that says she totally agrees with that statement. I nod.

As Chase runs to the side of the road and jumps up on a gate, I yell again for him to stop. The bull with horns brushes by him as the cows head back for the middle of the road. The farmers go by in their vehicles and shake their fists at us.

"I can't believe you did that," I say to Chase. "The cows could have been hurt."

"The cows? You're worried about those cows? What about me?"

"What about you? You started it. You could have damaged them, and that's how the farmers make a living."

"Damaged cows, no way. They're tough, and I wasn't hurting anything. Calm yourself down. You get upset over the smallest things." He pulls up his shirt and flaps it to cool off.

I start walking again, avoiding the fresh cow pies in the middle of the road. He comes up behind me and reaches for my hand, but I pull away from him and lengthen my step. What an idiot. I was just starting to trust him again, and he pulls a stunt like this.

"Valerie..." He comes after me. "It's no big deal. We're fine, and the cows are fine. They run with cows all the time in Spain."

"That's run with bulls, and this is not Pamplona."

"Oh, come on, Valerie, YOLO."

I step into his space. "How about YODO? You Only Die Once."

I turn my back on him and use the scarf to blot the tears threatening to run down my face. It makes me so mad that I cry when I get angry. Why can't I just get angry? I'll not give him the satisfaction of knowing he made me cry.

The Spanish girls have taken the opportunity to get ahead of us. They're turning the corner. I pick up my pace and practically run downhill. I'd like to stay near them and lose Chase, but we already have beds tonight in Unquera/Bustio at the donativo.

Chase catches up to me but remains silent. Let's see who can win this contest.

CHAPTER 9

UNQUERA/BUSTIO TO POÓ

The Spanish girls have just crossed the river Deva and are waiting on the other side. Crossing over the bridge, I see what has captivated them. It's a statue of a young female pilgrim. She has long braids, just like me. The plaque reads:

Ayuntamiento de Ribadeva
"Haciendo el Camino"
Autori R. Alzola Julio 2022

Translation: Ribadeva Town Hall
"Making the Way" Author R. Alzola July 2022
The sculpture is by Ramón Alzola

Chase breaks the silence. "Valerie, did you pose for that statue and not tell anyone?"

"Oh yes," I say and pose beside her. Chase takes pictures of us together. I give him my camera to take my picture too. "It's so cool that they have this statue of a young woman on the Camino. It's so modern, not like all the ancient religious statues. This town must really welcome its pilgrims."

"Sí. Vamos," Isabel says.

"Before we go, I'd like to get a picture of all three of you with her." Chase motions to us.

We lock arms and pose with the statue commemorating young female pilgrims. Chase immediately shares the photo with each of us. We keep our arms locked together as we start down the sidewalk to our albergue. Chase follows.

After a glass or two of wine at the community meal, Chase apologizes to me. He even admits to being an ass. We are making progress. I guess all couples fight.

. . .

Chase and I are on the road early. Leaving the Spanish girls at the albergue.

Of course, it's a steep climb out of town. The sun is already promising to make it a hot day. We take the coastal path along the cliff edge instead of the inland road, hoping for cool sea breezes and maybe a beach to take a dip.

The path turns into a narrow cow trail as it winds its way

between sinkholes created by the pounding surf. I stand at the edge of one of those holes. It's a long way down. If someone fell, they could never climb out. It makes me feel a bit dizzy.

I step back from the edge and look towards the sea. A cow stands on a limestone bridge carved out by the pounding surf. Only in Spain. I snap a quick picture.

Chase and I turn away from the sea and follow the path as it weaves between sinkholes. Then we descend an incline to a turquoise pool, which has sand along its edges.

"Let's go swimming," Chase suggests.

"That sounds lovely, but I don't have a suit."

"Just go in your underclothes. You'll dry in no time." He takes off his hiking boots and unzips his pants. I turn my back.

This is so idiotic. I see guys on the beach in swim trunks all the time. I wear a bikini, for God's sake. I drop my pack in the sand, pull my shirt over my head, and slip out of my shorts. In my running top and panties, I dash into the pool up to my waist. The water is so clear and cold that nothing is left to the imagination.

Chase dives in beside me. He comes up yelling and spraying water all over the place. He calls me a chicken, then grabs me and starts to submerge me.

"Stop," I scream. "I don't want to get my hair wet. It takes too long to dry."

"Excuses, excuses. You're cold," he says, looking at my chest.

"Well yeah, the water's cold."

"Race you to the other side," he yells and takes off swimming. I follow, doing a sedate breaststroke and keeping my head out of the water. He easily smokes me.

We walk up the beach to the limestone walls on this side of the sink. We explore a shallow cave, but there are no cave paintings here. We come back out into the sun, and the only way out of the sink is to wade into the water and swim back to our packs.

Chase takes his towel out of his pack and dries off. He grabs an orange and stretches out, using his pack for a headrest. I dry off and stretch out beside him. He hands me a section of orange. It's delicious.

Chase rolls over and kisses me. I can taste the fresh citrus on his lips. It's sexy. We're skin-to-skin. I snuggle close to soak in his warmth. The kiss deepens, and his hands make their way down my back. He cups my bottom, and my body responds. My nipples harden against his chest. I can feel his hardness through his wet underwear.

Oh no, do I really want to go there? It would be so easy. But I have never allowed a guy to penetrate me, and I'm not sure I want to start now. I place my hands on his chest and push him away.

"What's wrong, Val?"

"Look, I'm just not ready for the next step."

"Don't you like me?"

"Yes, I like you. But sometimes you scare me. I just don't want to lose my virginity on a beach in Spain."

"Sounds romantic to me," he says. "You're a virgin?"

"Yes, I told you that at the church with the Black Madonna."

"Oh, I didn't realize you meant you."

"Well, I did." I get up and grab my shorts.

"Here, let me brush the sand off before you put those on, or you will be miserable walking." He picks up his towel and starts to brush me off.

The towel against my skin is erotic. I've got to get a grip.

"Feel good," he says and smiles at me. "You are so sexy. I just can't believe how lucky I am to have met you on the plane. You are rocking my Camino."

Heat rushes into my cheeks. I dance away from him and put on my shorts. "You're rocking mine too. In fact, you are rocking my whole world."

He pulls on his shorts. "Better?"

"Well, yes and no," I say and step in for another kiss. It feels safer with some clothes between us.

"Look, if we can't complete the deed, you better not be playing with fire." He steps back, picks up my shirt, and hands it to me.

I put on my shirt and pin my towel to the outside of my pack to dry. Sitting down on a nearby rock, I put on my shoes, hiding my face from him. His disappointment is obvious. Damn. Things were going so well today, and then this ruins it all. I want to do it, but not like this. I always thought it would be more romantic and...uh...clean. Not sandy and gritty.

He reaches out his hand to help me up. We climb up the short slope to the path.

"So, how did the lady in the shop in Santillana like your video?" I ask.

"She loved it and all the hits I'm getting. I hope to get a few more gigs like that to pay for the trip. I'm getting a little low on funds."

"I hear you. I'm spending more money than I expected. There's a cheap albergue in Llanes, and we can stay there," I say, consulting my guidebook.

"I was thinking about camping on the beach. It would be so cool to sleep out here under the stars."

"Do they allow that?"

"Isn't it better to be forgiven than to have someone say no?" Chase says with a wink.

He's got that mischievous look back in his twinkling blue eyes, but he did respect my 'no.'

"Who's going to see us anyway?" he says.

"You have a point. They probably don't patrol the beaches. There's one just out of Llanes by the alternate Camino route along the beach. We can go grab some groceries for dinner."

"I'm so glad we ghosted the girls and Carl. I like it, just the two of us."

"I like it, too," I say.

We blow through Llanes, only stopping to get our credentials stamped at the church and buy some groceries. The beach is surrounded by a sea wall, and nothing is private about it. In fact, there are beach umbrellas and sunbathers everywhere.

We look at each other and say, "No" at the same time.

Chase consults his phone and says we can take the Coastal Senda route. A private beach is about four more clicks away.

I grab his hand. "Vamos."

We find the next arrow and follow the road to Póo. Really? A town named Póo? I'm sure it's pronounced differently in Spanish, but I still giggle.

Outside of town, there's a sign for the Costa Senda pointing to a dirt path through a copse of trees. We follow the winding path towards the coast, sharply descending to a well-worn path that leads to the small beach. The warm breeze is welcoming. I stop and remove the scarf from around my neck. Chase heads down the path to the beach.

I survey the crescent-shaped beach. Scrub trees come down to the rocks which create the boundary between sand and sea. There is one way in and one way out.

Chase waves at me to encourage my descent to the beach. I wave the scarf back at him. It flies in the breeze, and I make my descent. He had dropped his pack on a convenient flat rock. I drop mine and run across the beach.

"This is perfect." He takes me in his arms, and we waltz across the sand. "Let's explore for the perfect place to camp for the night. It's a small beach, but the woods and rocks surrounding it look promising." He spins me away and walks towards an outcropping of rocks.

I reach to touch the scarf. It's become a habit, and I thank Helen for encouraging me on this adventure. It's gone. I look around and pat myself down. No scarf.

"Chase, the scarf is gone. I just had it. You have to help me find it."

He calls back from the rock outcropping. "Over here looks promising."

"I'm retracing my steps."

"Valerie, it's just an old scarf. We need to find a place to set up camp."

"What? You are shitting me. It's not just an old scarf." My anger towards him quickly surfaces. I must not be over all the other shenanigans he has pulled. I run back to where

I dropped my pack. Maybe it got caught up in the straps when I took the pack off.

It's not there.

"Valerie, grab the packs and come over here. I think I found the perfect place."

I ignore him and retrace my steps up the path. There's a bit of red and orange sticking out from the undergrowth. Breathing a sigh of relief, I reach for it. It moves. I lunge forward and grab the fringe. I tug. It tugs back. It must be caught on something. I keep tension on the fringe and get closer to the underbrush.

Two eyes look at me, then there's a bark. I drop the fringe and jump back. A large, blonde dog runs out from under the bush with the scarf in his mouth. He drops the scarf at my feet, and when I reach to pick it up, he grabs it.

"Drop it!"

He gives me a puzzled look, drops it at my feet again, and whimpers.

"Maeloc," a man calls.

The dog woofs in response and runs towards the voice, leaving my scarf on the sand.

A couple of boys materialize out of the woods. They look exactly alike, down to the first stubble of beards sprouting on their cheeks and a rash of pimples across their noses.

"Hi, I'm so sorry. Did he bother you?" one of the boys says.

"Well, he's a thief. He stole my scarf." I can hardly keep the smile off my face.

The boy gives the dog a stern look. "Maeloc, you know better than that."

The dog whimpers with an apology. He's so cute. I can't help but smile. I pick the scarf up off the sand and shake it out.

Chase walks up to us. "What's going on?"

"Well, Maeloc stole my scarf, and I was able to convince him to return it."

"He didn't do it to be malicious. He likes to play. Oh, I'm Chulainn, but they call me Cú, and this is Lugh. We're twins. Our sister is back at the camp."

We introduce ourselves, and I wrap the scarf securely around my neck. "Are you from around here? Your English is great."

"Thank you," Cú says. "Since we have our dog, we're not welcome in many albergues, so we rough it."

"We're going to rough it ourselves tonight. The beach and the evening are perfect," I say.

"We have a camp in a small clearing just off the path. Join us. Our sister is there heating up some dinner." "Let's go meet your sister," I quickly suggest. Chase looks at me like I have lost my mind. 'What about us?' is written all over his face.

As we grab our packs, I whisper, "We don't have to stay with them."

They lead us down a small path I hadn't noticed to a clearing between the boulders at the edge of the sand and trees. A young woman is crouched over a camp stove, stirring something in a pot. She straightens as we walk into camp. Maeloc goes and sits next to her. He's very protective.

Chase walks up to her, and Maeloc eyes him suspiciously and lets out a low growl. I step up next to Chase, and Maeloc lies down. I swear he grins at me. "I'm Valerie, and this is Chase, " I say, extending my hand.

The young woman introduces herself as Brigit. She takes my hand and turns it palm up, peers at it, looks at me, and smiles. She points to a place where we can put our packs and sleeping bags. I'm relieved and feel safe. However, I am not sure why. Chase has been nothing but kind and respectful these past few days.

Chase walks over to stand beside me and whispers, "This is not what I had in mind for a private beach party."

"I know, but they are kind, and it feels safe with them. I was a bit nervous camping on the beach by ourselves."

"Why? We're perfectly safe."

"I know, but somehow this feels right. There are no coincidences on the Camino. Didn't you say to be open to the experience?"

Maeloc comes over and rubs against my leg. I grab our food and put the bread, cheese, salchichón, and fruit on the rock beside Brigit, which she seems to be using as a table. This will be a nice addition to the feast she is cooking up in the pot.

Chase shrugs and pulls a bottle of wine out of his pack. He opens it while the brothers pull some short logs from the woods for seats. Brigit says grace. Chase and I both have cups and spoons in our packs, and we use these for the stew. It's delicious. Getting into the moment, Chase takes his scallop shell from his pack and fills it with wine. We all follow suit. I wonder if the ancient pilgrims shared what they had with each other as we are doing now.

"You all have such unusual names. What do they mean?" I ask.

"Our parents are all about ancient Celtic and Galician lore," Lugh answers. "Our last name is Doran, which means wanderer. They decided that we should be named accordingly. Lugh means 'he who shines.' He brings in the Harvest and is equated with abundance. He's also a Giant Killer." Lugh flexes his biceps, laughing.

"My brother's complete name is Cú Chulainn. He's named after a Celtic hero who has a dog, symbolizing loyalty, fierceness, and protective instincts. Brigit is a poet and a healer with strength and wisdom. Maeloc was a bishop who connected the natural and the spiritual worlds. He guided people who were displaced by invaders through the mist. And it's just a really cool name."

"Where are you all from?" I ask.

"We are citizens of the world," Cú tells me.

"So is Chase," I tell them, glancing over at him. "That's amazing. Though he was born in the U.S."

"We were born in Ireland, but our parents have traveled, lectured, and studied all over the world. We're not exempt from their adventures. Currently, we're living in Santiago, where they have a shop near the cathedral. They put us on a train to Irún a few weeks ago and said, 'See you in Santiago.' It's kind of an initiation. What's your background?"

"My father was from Kenya, and my mom is from the U.S."

Bridgit finally speaks. "Was?"

Her chiming in surprises me. I've been wondering if she had a voice.

"Yes, he died when I was young," I tell her. "Sometimes I really miss him." Tears spring into my eyes. I can't stop them, and they run down my cheeks. I grab the end of the scarf and start blotting my face.

Brigit moves next to me, takes my hand, and gets a far-off look in her eyes. "Let the tears flow and honor him. He was a king among men. He would so admire the woman you have become. He followed his passion. You must follow yours."

Her touch and words are so comforting, but I still choke on my words between sobs. "This is really embarrassing. I don't know what is wrong with me. He died a long time ago."

"It's the Camino. As we walk, we release our pain. You must allow it to be released. The pain of grief and abandonment is ruling your heart. Tears are a good way to release the pain."

The sobs come harder.

Chase stands up all of a sudden and pulls me away from Brigit. "Let's go. This is crazy. These people are crazy."

"No, Chase, I'm ok. I just didn't realize I had so much grief. We're safe here."

"Are you sure?" he says, enveloping me in a hug.

"We won't harm you," Lugh says. "Brigit has a gift of seeing into people and sometimes it's a bit hard to take. She doesn't mean any harm."

I untangle myself from Chase and reach for Brigit's hand. "It's all right. I so appreciate your words. Sometimes I think I must have been a disappointment to my father, being born defective, and he was so strong."

She brings her hand to my cheek. "Never a disappointment. You have his strength and your mother's love and kindness."

Her gentle hand on my cheek spreads warmth throughout my body. "Yes, it's all right. I needed this confirmation." I smile at Chase. "Thank you for bringing me to this place."

"Come look at the sky," Lugh calls to us as he and Cú take off for the beach to get a clearer view of the sky. The sun is sinking behind the headland at the end of the beach and lighting up the clouds in a burst of oranges, reds, and purples. "It's the colors of your scarf."

I lean against Chase who has walked up behind me and encircled me in his arms. Content, I walk back to the clearing with him and stake out a place for our sleeping bags. He unrolls his sleeping bag next to mine as the last of the light disappears. Maeloc wiggles his way between us and settles down to sleep.

CHAPTER IO

POÓ TO VILLAVIACOSA

Awake now, we all break camp and walk back up the path. At the top of the bluff, we head west to the town of Celorio, hoping to find coffee and a bathroom. We take care of our morning needs and stop at the local grocery. There's a place on the side of the building where Brigit clips Maeloc's leash. I had noticed these rings before but didn't realize that they were for dog leashes.

Brigit comes out of the grocery, puts a bag of dog food in the small pack over Maeloc's back, and takes out some leather booties. I wondered about this pack when she buckled it onto him this morning. He sits and gives her a paw one at a time, so she can secure the booties to his feet. She turns to me and smiles.

"They protect his feet on the roads and rocky paths. He carries his food and water bowl in the saddle bag on his back."

Lugh and Chase consult their maps and guides and determine that a donativo is about twenty klicks ahead at the top of a mountain. We make our way over dirt paths through the woods and, at times, we walk alongside the highway on asphalt.

We pass through the town of Piñeres de Pria and take the farm road indicated by the next yellow arrow. The road takes us beside a huge field that sits in front of a church. There are a couple of pilgrims trudging through the field. The cows are too interested in grazing to bother with the pilgrims invading their fields. We follow them up the muddy path made even more slippery by the fresh cow dung. I try to avoid it, but it's all over the place.

At the end of the path is the church and a small rectory. A couple of pilgrims sit on the porch of the rectory and wave us in. We remove our shoes outside and put them in the cubbies provided. After checking in, we stake out our beds and return to the porch. The priest says that Maeloc can sleep in the barn behind the rectory.

We shower and go down for the community dinner. How quickly things can change. Chase and I were going to have a special night on the beach, but it became special in an unexpected way. Tonight, we're with new friends and a dog on a mountaintop, sharing a meal at a church.

Dinner finished, I wander over to the church. Shaking out the scarf, I wrap it around my shoulders like a shawl.

The church is simple, and in a way, I prefer this to the elaborate cathedrals. I slip into a pew and express my gratitude. Peace envelops me. I feel my father's presence. It feels as if he wants me to know that all is well and he has never abandoned me, even in death. I hug the scarf close, and it's as if he has his arms around me.

Someone softly calls my name. I don't know how long I have been sitting there. I turn, and a priest beckons me to the back of the church. He motions for me to leave as he turns and locks the doors. We walk in silence back to the albergue.

I make my way into the dormitory and get ready for bed. Chase is already snoring in his bunk. He had a restless night last night. I don't think he was too pleased that Maeloc came between us. Actually, I'm relieved it happened that way. Slipping into bed, I snuggle with the scarf and close my eyes to sleep.

· · ·

The bright sun streaming through the window wakes me up. The dormitory is empty. I quickly complete my morning routine, then grab coffee and toast from the kitchen and pack my bag. Chase is waiting for me by the front door, smiling. I don't see the Doran family or Maeloc. Chase says they have gone ahead.

A road leads away from the church, and it soon turns into a path which plunges as we get close to Ribadesella. We walk into town through narrow streets with ancient walls. Some of the stones in the walls stick out, leading to steps that go up into someone's postage stamp-sized yard.

We emerge from the narrow streets into a plaza on the waterfront, where the roar of the crowd welcomes us. Laughing, I bow to them. Chase joins in, curtseying and giving the royal wave.

But it's not for us. Their enthusiasm is for a rowing competition of some sort. We make our way through the crowd to the edge of the wharf. There are many small boats being paddled along a course on the river. A spectator tells me that this town is famous for its rowers and the competition. The rowers start seventeen kilometers upriver in Arriondas and row their canoes down to the finish line, just off the wharf in Ribadesella.

Chase wanders away, and I cheer with the crowd when the next two teams come in. Chase comes back with a pizza he bought at a local shop. We find a bench to sit on and eat as we watch more rowers come down the river to the finish line.

I search the name of the town on my phone. It's not only famous for rowing but has some of the most ancient cave paintings ever discovered.

"OMG, I heard about these on National Geographic. The Tito Bustillo Cave is here," I tell Chase. I consult the map in my guidebook. The cave is just across the river. "Let's go look."

"Do you paddle a boat?" Chase asks.

"I don't think we need a boat. We can just walk across the bridge to the caves." I wink at him.

"No, I mean, there's an opportunity here for us. They have to have sports stores that sell this rowing equipment. Let's go see if we can make them go viral. My followers just love you. Come on."

"Okay, then after that, can we go visit the caves?"

"We'll see," he says, shouldering his pack. He walks toward the town center and disappears into a shop while I stand outside watching the crowd.

I understand that he needs to make a living—this is his job—and I need to support him. But I would love to see those caves. I can't believe we're right here. I never thought I would be so close to something that National Geographic takes seriously.

"Valerie, come here," Chase calls from the door of a shop. "This is Pedro, the owner of this rowing shop. He said he'll let me publicize his shop on YouTube. He loves what you did in the surfing video. He wants you to get out on the water in one of his boats. We'll video you on the water talking about his equipment."

"I only see one problem here. I have never rowed one of those boats before."

"It's easy," Pedro says, leering at me. "I hear you're a Florida girl. I'm sure you have rowed a boat."

That feeling of creepy crawls up my spine. I tell him I've kayaked with friends before, moving closer to Chase for protection.

"Same thing. You don't have to be an expert. You just have to look pretty in the picture. We're trying to attract a more diverse crowd, and you're perfect."

There is something about that statement that feels so totally wrong.

"Come on, Valerie..." Chase looks at me with those big blue eyes. "For me?"

I acquiesce. I mean, how bad can this be, paddling a boat around in a swimsuit?

I follow Pedro and Chase into the shop. Pedro picks out a skimpy bikini and shows me the dressing room. "I'll meet you across the street at the dock. Our rentals are there."

I put on the suit and cover it up with my hiking shorts and top. At the dock, Pedro gives me a quick lesson. I strip down to the suit. They film me getting into the boat and then paddling away from the dock.

"*Mira*," someone yells in Spanish.

I look up from my paddle. A large boat is approaching.

I panic and try to paddle backwards, but I hit a boat behind me.

"Estúpido," someone else yells. I don't need a translator for that.

I freeze, not sure which way to go. The river is covered with boats, but at least I'm not near the finish line. Someone grabs the back of my boat and pulls me next to them.

A woman with a kind face asks, "Principiante? Beginner?"

"Sí," I reply, shaking. What was I thinking, letting Chase talk me into this?

"Mira," she says, telling me to look, then she indicates that I need to put on the life jacket tucked under the bungee cord on the front of the boat. She then shows me how to hold the double-ended paddle and gives me a quick lesson.

She motions for me. I follow her along the edge of the wharf. There is less traffic, and the river is not as churned up. We find a quiet eddy and practice turning. She smiles, gives me a thumbs up, and goes back to join her friends.

Once you know how to handle the paddle, it isn't too hard. I head back toward the dock where Chase is filming.

"Take off the jacket," Chase demands when I get close to the dock. I put the paddle across the front of the boat and take off the jacket. I slip it under the bungee and, in doing so, dislodge the paddle. It slides into the water. As I reach for it, I flip the boat.

I come up for air and yell, "Shit!" The water is fucking cold. I grab onto the upside-down boat and search for the paddle that's floating a few feet away. Letting go of the boat, I swim for the paddle. That located, I turn to look for the boat.

"What's the idiot doing?" Pedro asks loud enough for me to hear.

"She's acting. This makes a great video. People will love this," Chase tells him.

"She makes my boat and paddle look like a joke."

"Just watch. It'll be great once edited," Chase replies.

Instead of talking about the commercial, they should be rescuing me. I hold the paddle out in front of me and kick my legs to get me closer to the boat.

A couple of other paddlers come to my rescue. They right the boat and take the paddle. Holding the boat steady, I pull myself in. Gooseflesh covers me, and I'm shivering. They indicate the life jacket, and I put it back on. Then they hand me the paddle. I come alongside the dock.

Pedro holds the boat as I get out. Chase is filming the whole time. "Now turn to the camera, remove the life jacket, and talk about Pedro's shop."

"Well, at least Pedro came to help me. You're just standing there filming. I could have been drowning, and you would have kept on filming."

"Oh, Valerie. Just be dramatic for the camera."

I turn to Pedro and thank him for helping me. I give him a huge smile for the camera. It's not his fault that I got into this mess. I take off the life jacket and hand it to Pedro. He puts his arm around me. His hand is draped over my shoulder, a little too close to my chest for comfort, and he looks into the camera.

"We take care of our students from beginner to advanced," he says without missing a beat. He turns and smiles at my chest, which has reacted embarrassingly to the cold.

Aware we are on camera, I step back from him and grab the life jacket. "I'm ready to try again," I say and put the life jacket on. I grab the paddle and gingerly get back into the boat. I push myself off the dock and go paddling around. The other boats make room for me. I execute a turn. Not as smoothly as I hoped, but I did turn. I paddle back to the dock.

I hand the paddle to Pedro, who helps me get back out of the boat. I then strip off the life vest, smile at the camera, and say, "How's that for drama?"

"You're awesome," Chase says, then he kisses me. He points me back to Pedro and raises the camera to film us.

I emote to the camera. "Pedro, thank you for this opportunity to learn about your wonderful sport. Your shop is the best in Ribadesella."

Now that we've finished filming, I make my way back to the shop, get a towel, and change back into my clothes. Do all models go through this?

Chase and Pedro have followed me back to the shop. Chase explains to Pedro that he will edit the video to make it commercial-worthy and asks for an advance.

"Find a place for us to stay tonight with Wi-Fi," Chase says to me.

I look up places on my app. There is an albergue just across the river. It only has eight beds. Chase tells me to go check in, and he'll meet me there. I grab my pack and make my way across the river while he finishes with Pedro.

. . .

Tonight, he is working on the video while I catch up on Facebook. It's been a while since I posted. I post pictures of our last couple of days and write a funny story about my rowing adventure and the caves in the area. I so want to see those caves. It's amazing that people who lived so long ago decorated their living spaces with art. It shows they had the time and energy to create.

Dot replies to my post about the caves: *I think you should go see those caves. The only regret I have in my long life is missing opportunities for really insignificant reasons. Please don't miss the opportunity. If I were there, I would go with you in a heartbeat.*

I reply: *I wish you were here to go with me. I'll send you a full report of my experience. Are you preparing for a Camino?*

Dot: *It's on my bucket list. And it has definitely moved higher following you. I would like to do it before I die.*

I reply: *Well, I hope you are not going to die soon.*

Dot: *When you're 75, you don't even buy ripe bananas. What's stopping you from seeing the caves?*

I reply: *Well, actually nothing. I was taking my walking buddy into account, but that doesn't mean I can't do what I want to do.*

Dot: *Darn, right. Go for it.*

I go find Chase, who's in the common room, working on the video.

"There's some good stuff here," he says when I walk in.

"I did what you wanted today. I want to go check out the caves in the morning."

"That's perfect. While you're checking out the caves, I'll show Pedro what I put together."

He turns back to his editing. I'm not sure it's a victory.

. . .

I head to the caves this morning. There's a tour starting at ten a.m., and they even have lockers where I can store my pack. I wander upstairs to the museum. It's truly amazing that people who had so little were able to create such magnificent tools and art.

On a high now that my tour is over, I go to Pedro's shop. Chase and Pedro look like best buddies. I'm glad that worked out.

Pedro approaches me and hugs me tight against his chest. It's still creepy.

I pull away and say, "Are you all done? It's getting late, and if we want to get to La Isla this evening, we better start walking."

"Why don't you go ahead, and I'll catch up. We have a couple of loose ends to tie up."

"Okay, it's a long walk, sixteen klicks, and very hilly. It's getting late," I remind him.

"Let's stay here. I bet they will let us stay another night at the albergue. Or Pedro, do you maybe have a suggestion where we can stay?"

"Look, Chase, I'm on a time limit," I say, now annoyed. "I, too, have a job and have to get back to the U.S. I really need to keep on schedule. We've already lost one afternoon of walking." I head towards the door. At least I got to see the caves. So what if Chase doesn't care about caves? He is very motivated by his work. That's a good thing.

"Tell you what, why don't you go ahead, get us a couple of beds, and I'll catch a bus. I might even get there before you do."

I walk down the street and score a grocery. I run in and grab some snacks for the road. Then I find the arrow, pointing me back over the bridge, and follow it out of town.

I wonder how the Dorans are doing. I haven't seen them since the rectory. It's strange how people come in and out of your life on this walk. Brigit was fascinating. Her ability to see into my heart is amazing. Since I was able to talk about my father with her and cry, I feel lighter somehow. I think about the doll he gave me that's hanging from my pack. It's like he has been with me every step of the way.

The road becomes steep as the arrows point me away from the coast towards the inland mountain range. What did Carl say? "Keep the sea on your right and the mountains on your left, and you can't go wrong."

It takes me about forty-five minutes to walk the five kilometers up the mountain to San Esteban de Leces. I stop at the summit and sit on a conveniently placed bench with a beautiful view.

The sun is warm on my face. I pull an orange and nuts out of my pack. The smell of the orange as I break it open transports me back to Florida. I close my eyes for a moment and wonder how Mom is doing. I wonder if Brigit would have some insight on her.

Something wet and cold bumps my leg, and I open my eyes.

"Maeloc." I scratch him between the ears. The Dorans walk up, and I jump up to hugs all around. "You all look bedraggled. Where did you spend the night last night?"

"We were just outside of Ribadesella. A farmer discovered us this morning and chased us off his property, where we were stealth camping. We're headed to La Isla to the albergue. We hope we can keep Maeloc with us," Brigit says.

"I'll put in a good word for him. I'm headed that way too."

"Where's Chase?" Lugh asks.

"He's finishing some business in Ribadesella and will be along soon."

"Walk with us."

"I'd love to." I offer orange sections all around and put the peel in my garbage bag, which I'll throw in the next trash bin.

We encounter many ups and downs, forest paths, and roads. We wander into La Isla, a small town situated along a highway, and wind our way through the back streets toward the beach. The arrows take us past a grocery store, and we mark the spot in our minds. Finally, an albergue on the edge of town by the ocean. Brigit and I go to check in and get beds.

"I need two beds," I tell the hospitalero.

She launches into a tirade of Spanish. I look at Brigit.

"You cannot save a bed for someone who is not here," she says. "You can only reserve your own bed. She's been skunked too many times."

"Oh, what should I do?" I ask Brigit.

"Go ahead and reserve a bed for you."

I take out my money to pay.

"I'll go out and relieve the boys, and they will come in and get two beds," she says when we go in and stake out a bed. "One of us will have to stay outside with Maeloc. I don't think she will welcome him. Then, that way, we'll have a bed for Chase."

"Good idea. I'll give you the cash for his bed."

As far as Maeloc is concerned, they're subscribing to Chase's rule that it's better to be forgiven than say no.

Brigit and I go back to the grocery store while the boys take turns keeping Maeloc out of sight and taking showers. We cook a pot of noodles and tomato sauce, take it to a vacant lot overlooking the ocean, and eat. I make sure we have a serving left for Chase.

Still no Chase. I wonder if this is how he felt when I ghosted him. I'm wondering if he's ghosting me after the mess I made of his video. I think they were just being kind to me. I'm not an actress. I'm a nurse.

The sun drops, and the hospitalero leaves for the night. The boys sneak Maeloc into the courtyard and tie his leash to a post where he can get under cover of the porch and also access the grass in the yard.

My phone dings. It's a text from Chase: I have another opportunity, and I'll meet you at the albergue in Villaviciosa.

Lugh asks if he can eat Chase's portion. A growing boy needs many calories, so he heats it up and shares it with Cú. They have this down pat.

. . .

It's morning, and Brigit is already up and out. She must be dog-sitting. The boys and I eat the standard toast and coffee. I make a jelly sandwich for the road with the apple and cheese I bought at the grocery store. I have plenty.

We leave the albergue. Brigit and Maeloc are waiting for us beside a pasture. Since we only have twenty-one klicks to go, we set a leisurely pace and wander up and down the hills. The boys are whispering amongst themselves. Cú comes up to me. His face is red.

"Did you know that Chase is posting your video online?"

"Yes, we did a video for his client in Ribadesella about rowing. Why?"

"Have you seen it?"

"No."

"He shows you coming out of the water. It's like a wet t-shirt video, only more revealing."

"What? No way. I had a swimsuit on and a life jacket. It was for a YouTube rowing advertisement."

"Did he pay you?"

"No, I didn't get paid. The other two times when he did advertising on YouTube videos, he would spring for a beer or dinner. I don't think he makes much. He never seems to have any money."

"I didn't see it on YouTube. It's on PornNow."

"Wait. What? What's PornNow?"

"You know what porn is?"

"Well yeah. Like magazines that men like. Wait... how do you know it's me?"

"Well, this is online, and they just say the first names of the ladies. The ladies are doing all sorts of sexual things."

"I haven't had sex with anyone, so it can't be me."

"Sometimes it's just naked pictures."

"I haven't been naked in front of a camera either."

There's no way this could be me. I haven't done anything remotely provocative. Chase wouldn't do this to me anyway. He has treated me with respect. Yeah, there have been a couple of close calls, but there was no camera involved. And it's only natural when two people really like each other.

"I'll send you the link when we get to a place that has Wi-Fi."

"Thank you. But I'm sure you are wrong."

"Well, it sure looks like you, and I haven't seen too many women who look like you on this Camino."

"And what are you doing browsing porn sites anyway?" I ask.

"Well, s-sometimes the nights in the yard with Maeloc feel really long. Chase told me about the site. B-but he didn't say anything about you," he stammers.

"Valerie, come help. Maeloc has gotten into some thorns, and I can't get them out." There's panic in Brigit's voice.

Cú and I rush to where Lugh and Brigit hold onto a miserable-looking Maeloc. I drop my pack, open it, and search for my tweezers and first aid kit. I give Brigit the scarf to wrap around Maeloc to swaddle him so I can work on his feet. The poor guy has made a mess of himself.

"What happened?"

"He dashed into the undergrowth after a rabbit, and I heard him yelp. I called him, and he came out limping."

While they hold him, I remove the thorns from his feet. I look around for the dock leaf plant. It's amazing. It grows beside nettles. It's like Mother Nature has the cure next to the malady.

I make a poultice of the dock leaf and water. I ask for Maeloc's booties and put the poultice inside, then put them on him. Dock leaf should help thorns too. It can't hurt. He looks at me in relief and licks me in gratitude.

"Why wasn't he wearing his booties?" I ask.

"I only use them for road walking, so they won't wear out so soon."

"That's fair," I say. She seems to feel guilty enough without me adding to it. "Brigit, it's all right, accidents happen. Let him rest for a moment and get some relief before he starts walking again."

"Can you help me too? I got into nettles when I was grabbing for Maeloc."

I make another poultice for her and wrap it onto her hand with her bandana.

Maeloc gingerly tries to walk. Soon, he is moving forward unimpeded. We shoulder our packs and follow him.

I just can't get the idea of that video out of my mind. It can't be me. Chase wouldn't do this to me without asking my permission. He knows I would tell him no way. But didn't he say once that he doesn't ask for permission, just forgiveness?

I grab a hold of the scarf. Oh, shit, am I ever an idiot. I fell for him and his scam. It was right there in front of my face all the time. I thought he was on the level.

Maybe it wasn't him. Maybe it was that creepy Pedro. Maybe he and Pedro are working together. That's why he's staying in Ribadesella. He can just stay there as far as I am concerned.

I take the scarf off and hug it. "Oh, Helen, I just don't know what to do." Tears blur my eyes, and I wipe them with the scarf.

CHAPTER 11

VILLAVIACOSA TO GIJÓN

The path turns into a road as we walk into the city of Villaviciosa. It's the largest city in the area. Shops and apartments line the road, and the noise of the traffic is assaulting my ears. We get closer to the center, and Cú puts Maeloc on a leash.

The cafes spill tables onto the sidewalks, and people are enjoying the afternoon sun and repast. A waiter steps out of a doorway with a bottle and a glass. He holds the bottle as high as he can in one hand and pours an amber liquid into a glass that he holds as low as he can with the other hand.

He turns to me and says, "A sidra for you?"

"A what?"

"Sidra, in English, is cider. We are famous for it. It's best when poured from a great height to keep the fizz and prevent the sediment from entering the glass. We discard the sediment in the bottom of the bottle." He shows me the empty bottle and there's the sediment. He then turns the bottle upside down and shakes the sediment out into the street. He looks at me questionably.

"No, ahora, no, gracias," I say, letting some Spanish slip into my vocabulary. I smile at him and see the Dorans ahead of me on the grass of a park in front of what looks like a town hall. Cú is consulting his phone.

Lugh sees me and waves. "Valerie, we are trying to find a place to stay, but no one will allow Maeloc. We will have to walk to the outskirts of town and find a place to camp."

I'm torn. I would like to go with them, but Chase said he would catch up with me. Also, I need to get on Wi-Fi and check out the links Cú is sending me.

"I better stay here. There is an albergue just across the street, and I need to talk to Chase. He's supposed to be meeting me here."

We share hugs all around, and they leave. I go back to the cafe, find a seat where I can watch pilgrims walking into town, and order a sidra and an ensalada mixa. The waiter comes and pours my drink from on high. A couple of ladies with backpacks stop and stare. I motion for them to join me. They take off their packs, and each orders a sidra.

"We were just reading about this being the cider town. Thank you for asking us to join you. The seats are going fast."

"Where did you walk from?"

"We stayed at a hotel in La Isla last night. We prefer to stay in hotels to hostels, but at our age, we can afford it. Besides, Spain is cheap compared to Norway."

"And warmer too," her companion says. "Where are you from?"

"Florida, but I walked in from La Isla today. I stay as cheap as possible."

"Ah, to be young again."

My ensalada mixa arrives, and it's huge. It's on a bed of lettuce with three stalks of white asparagus, quarters of tomato, and a sliced hard-boiled egg. Fresh flaked tuna is on the side, and onions are sprinkled on top. The waiter returns with a basket of bread and a small carafe of olive oil.

The ladies say in unison, "I'll have what she's having." We all laugh.

The waiter brings out more sidra and then returns with their salads.

This Camino is amazing. Just when you think you are all alone, wonderful people appear.

We eat and order another sidra. I have another thirty minutes to kill before I can check in. We compare Camino notes, and they say they're ending their Camino in Gijon, thirty kilometers on. They will stay the night in Gijón and get a taxi to the airport in Avilés the next morning. It would have been nice to walk with them for a while. I have to get off this Chase merry-go-round.

We stand, and as I lean over to grab my pack I lose my balance. One of the ladies grabs my arm. "Steady, that sidra packs a punch."

"Oh yes, it does."

"Are you all right to walk to your albergue?"

"Yeah, I was just light-headed there for a minute. It's just over there across the square." I shoulder my pack, and we cross the street. At the next corner, they depart to their hotel, and I walk, not too steadily, into the entrance of my albergue.

I hope no one notices I'm a little buzzed. I walk up to the reception desk. A woman of color greets me. She exudes confidence and class. Not someone you would want to mess with. In response, I straighten myself up and ask for a bed. She consults her chart and then looks straight at me.

Oh, no. She knows I'm drunk. She won't let me in here. I'm such a loser.

"The scarf you're wearing looks so familiar. Where did you get it?"

Oh God, I hope she doesn't think I stole it.

"My friend Helen gave it to me for my Camino. She found it on hers and said it had to come back to the Camino."

"Helen? Nurse Helen from Tampa?"

"Well, yes, I think so. We're in nursing school together.

She's older and walked the Camino last year with a group of Catholic women."

The woman comes from around the desk and hugs me tight.

"Who are you?" I ask as I look her over. She's black like me and has curly, cropped hair with streaks of gray. She looks fit.

"Oh, sorry. Helen is such a special lady, and you have to be special too, for her to have given you the scarf. I'm Emily. We walked the French route together. This is amazing."

"Oh my God. It's so awesome to meet you. You're the one who wants to be Pope."

Emily laughs. "Well, I'm not sure I want to be Pope, but I believe women should have the opportunity if they desire the job. Let's get you a bed. Then we'll go have a bite to eat and talk. I want to hear all about you and Helen."

I follow her upstairs to a dorm with about ten bunks. She shows me to an empty top bunk in the corner that has a plug. All the other bunks are taken. She looks at me apologetically.

"This is about all we have left. There are many pilgrims on the way right now. Oh, and the Wi-Fi code is on the back of the door." She lowers her voice. "Bring your dirty clothes down with you, and I'll get them washed."

I don't care. A bed is a bed, and laundry is laundry. I've hit the jackpot. It's amazing how much the little things mean, and tears well up in my eyes. I drop my pack on the floor, and we agree to meet downstairs in an hour.

I hook into the Wi-Fi, and there's a text from Chase: Sorry for another delay. This guy is keeping me busy. I owe you. See you soon.

I owe you. What does that mean? I reply with a thumbs-up, letting him know that I got the message. I just don't know what to say.

I have messages from Cú with the links to the porn sites. Lying in my bunk, not wanting to move, I start checking them.

There has to be a mistake. But no, there it is. I'm stepping out of the kayak, stark naked, onto the dock in slow motion. There is no swimsuit or life jacket. How can that be? I pause and zoom in. It sure looks like my face and body. Then there's another one advertising the beaches and turquoise pools. I am leaning over, splashing water on my body, and it's running down my naked back. I had my underwear on at this pool. This is not cool. I switch over to YouTube, and on Chase's channel, there's a video of me wearing a swimsuit and a life jacket in a kayak. This is legit, and I'm okay with it. But the other...

I call him on WhatsApp. Yeah, he owes me. He owes me an explanation, and he has to take this down. It goes straight to voicemail. Maybe he's on a bus on his way here.

I can't believe he would do this to me. There has to be a way to block it.

Emily is locking up the register at the front desk when I approach with my laundry. She grabs it and disappears into the back room. She walks back out with her fanny pack, and we head out for some food.

"This is the best local place in town for a meal. They have an awesome sidra. You should try some. It's the local specialty."

The thought of more sidra makes me want to gag. I let her know that I already had my fill earlier and I'll take an Aquarius. She orders some tapas and bread.

"So tell me how you know Helen and why you have the scarf. You know that's a very special scarf."

I run my hand over the scarf and let my hand stop on my heart where the scarf ends. Thank you, I say silently. You brought me to Emily.

I tell her the story of meeting Helen in school and how she tutors me in math. "I'm so honored to be wearing her scarf and to know her. She's a very special lady." My eyes fill again with tears.

"What's wrong?" Emily asks.

"I'm such an idiot," I blurt out. "I met this guy on the plane, and he convinced me to walk the Norte with him. Now he's using me in his online business without my permission."

"What kind of business?"

"I thought it was just YouTube advertising videos, but he also has a porn site. A guy that we were walking with showed it to me this morning. I'm so ashamed. I could lose everything I have worked for. My mom's going to be devastated when she finds out, not to mention Helen and my school."

"Slow down. Let me make sure I've got this. This guy has been taking videos of you and posting them on a porn site. You must have realized this when he was taking video when you were nude."

"That's just the point. I was wearing a swimsuit. I wasn't naked. I'd never do that."

"Were you under the influence when he videoed you?"

"No, I wasn't. I only drank too much sidra today because I didn't know what else to do. He's supposed to be bussing in to catch up with me, but he keeps telling me that he's been delayed."

"Did you know that there is an app that uses AI to undress a person?"

"What...? How do you know this?"

"I work in IT. AI has many wonderful applications, but it also has a dark side."

"Please help me." I can't believe this. "How can we get rid of it?"

"I believe there may be a way. I'll do some checking."

"Thank you so much. I'm so sorry for dragging you into this." I'm such a loser. She doesn't even know me. "If you work in IT, what are you doing working in an albergue?"

Emily laughs. "I'm a volunteer. I spend two weeks of my vacation giving back to the Camino as a volunteer, and then I walk. It's my time to renew."

Her laughter puts me at ease. "I get that. But I wasn't trying to renew myself as a porn star." I suck in a deep breath and slowly let it out. "I came to see if I could walk a Camino. I was 'called.' That's what Helen said."

"Yes, we don't always know why we are called. When I walked, I totally thought I was going to be out of a job when I got back from my Camino. But instead, this amazing consulting opportunity came my way. I can work when I want to as long as I make my deadlines. And I can take time off for myself. It's the best of both worlds."

"How cool is that? Chase says he works as an influencer because he can work when he wants to and take time for travel too. I was so envious. I just wanted to help him with his business. He said I was such a natural in front of the camera, and the videos he put up of me were going viral. I'm such a loser."

"No, you're not. You're a woman with a kind heart who's been taken advantage of. We're going to fix this.

No woman, ever, should be taken advantage of. There are laws to protect you."

We walk back to the albergue. "Let's call Helen on WhatsApp. It's three o'clock in the afternoon in Florida," Emily suggests. "We won't say anything about the internet issue."

It's so fun listening to Helen and Emily reminisce. They pull me into their circle of women who walk the Camino. Helen promises to let my mom know that I am in good hands.

"Now, let's report this to the police," Emily says.

"The police? Oh my God. Will they think I asked for it? That I knew what I was doing?"

"You're blessed to be in Asturias, Spain. This province respects its matriarchal roots. You have noticed the number of Virgin Mary statues everywhere?" She smiles and squeezes my hand. "Women are treated with respect, and people who disrespect women are subject to penalty."

I nod and start playing with my braids. I haven't done that in forever, and I remove my hands from my hair and put them in my pocket.

"Remember, you're the victim here. Don't let him keep you a victim. You must stand up for yourself and all the other women that have been hurt too by men misusing their identity."

"OMG. Emilia. I wonder if he did the same thing to her. You're right. But are they going to believe me? I'm so ashamed."

"Who's Emilia?"

"She's a woman we walked with at the beginning, and we went surfing together. Chase videoed us for a surfing commercial." I quickly scroll through my phone and find her Emilia's contact information.

"Yes, the evidence is online. And don't be ashamed. He sexually abused you. And possibly your friend Emilia. That is not all right."

I sigh, thinking it through. "Okay. You're right. He may have done this to other women. I don't want this to happen to anyone else."

We make the call. The policeman is so kind. He says this isn't the first time a young woman has been compromised, and he's glad I haven't been physically hurt. I give him Emilia's contact information. We make a plan for the police to bring Chase in for questioning once I find out exactly where he is.

I feel so much better. Emily hugs me and says she will have my clothes ready for me at breakfast.

Now in bed, I check my messages. I text Emilia and let her know what's happened and that I have contacted the police.

Emilia texts back: *I looked at the site and don't see myself.*
Thank you for the heads up. I was right. He is possessed.
I will talk to the police in case a video is posted of me later.

I'm so glad she hasn't been compromised.

Chase had sent a message saying he would meet me in Gijón and make reservations for us at a hotel. He sent the address and suggested I go there and wait for him.

My stomach clenches. I don't know how to respond. I'll talk to Emily about it in the morning before I say or do anything.

I call Mom and let her know where I am. She asks if I have made any friends. I tell her all about the scarf, Emily, and Helen. Then I let her know that I'm walking with the Doran siblings and their dog.

"I'm so proud of you," she says.

If she only knew.

"I love you, Mom," I say and hang up,

For comfort, I look at the picture of Emily and me with the scarf that the waiter took at the restaurant. Emily said I could post the pictures and the story about how we met on my Instagram and Camiga's Facebook page. I hug the scarf to my chest and close my eyes.

· · ·

True to her word, Emily has my clothes clean and folded. They smell so good. I put them in my pack, and we go to the community room for breakfast.

"What nationality is Chase?" Emily asks.

"He's American, though he says he's a 'citizen of the world.'" I can't keep the sarcasm out of my voice.

"That makes it easier. He is breaking the law here in Spain, and there is a penalty, especially since he is doing it for profit. You did say that he was making money from his videos, right?"

"Yes, that's right."

"Have you heard from him?"

"Yes, he told me that he has a hotel for us in Gijón and to meet him there."

"It's hard to face someone who has wronged you, especially someone you trusted and had feelings for. Can you stand up to him when the police confront him and then stand by it?"

"Yes. Will you come help me?"

"Let me see what I can do. I'm committed to the albergue, but I think you can stand up for yourself."

"If you can't make it physically, can I call you for support?"

"Of course, I'll do my best. Gijón is only thirty kilometers away, but it feels like a huge distance to a walker." She gently pulls on the end of the scarf around my neck and says, "You're not alone."

Her response helps to settle me down, and I take a deep breath.

"Now respond to his message and say, 'I'll meet you in Gijon. I'll be there this evening. When are you arriving?' Then call the police and let them know about the arrangements."

While I send the text and make the call, she gets up to assist some other pilgrims who have come in for breakfast. It feels so sneaky to betray him this way. What am I thinking? He betrayed me. I have to get my thinking straight, as Mom would say. What is Mom going to say when she finds out about this? It's just too overwhelming.

I distract myself with Facebook. My post has already received several positive responses. The lady, Dot, is especially excited. She said something about living vicariously through me on this pilgrimage. If she only knew.

My phone dings with a message. It's him.

"He responded," I tell Emily. "He says he will be in Gijón tomorrow on the afternoon bus and will meet me at the hotel."

"Just give him a thumbs up. You don't have to text back."

Emily checks the bus schedule on her phone, and then I call the policeman we spoke with last night. I give him my number, and he gives me his direct cell phone number. He reassures me that they will be waiting for the call.

"You know why so many women come to walk the Camino in Spain?" she asks me.

"Because they feel safe?"

"Yes, because they feel safe. We look out for our pilgrims. There are bad characters everywhere, but most know that this behavior will not be tolerated. Now Chase will have to learn his lesson. You just have to ask for help."

She hands me a bag containing a bocadillo and an orange. "This will help you get over the mountain today." She hugs me before she walks away.

I put the food in my pack and leave the albergue. I feel better than I have in several days.

Honestly, I knew something was off with Chase, but I wanted to believe in him. Is that a crime? He was so nice to me. I don't know his history or why he would do something like this. Maybe he doesn't even realize how damaging it is. He has been so respectful. Yeah, he has a temper, and yeah, he used me, but is he a criminal?

CHAPTER 12

GIJÓN TO SAN MARTÍN DE LASPRA

My right foot starts to hurt as I hobble into Gijón. I'm scared to take off my shoes and look. The GPS shows that it's less than a kilometer to the hotel. I can wait.

I approach the hotel, and my heart begins racing. I stop at a small cafe and message the policeman that I am in town. He tells me to go to the hotel to see if Chase has arrived and text him to let him know.

I walk up to the hotel's reception desk and give them my name. I ask if Chase has arrived, and she tells me that he is in the room. He had told the desk to expect me. I text the police this info with the room number. The officer suggests that I keep him busy in the room until they arrive. It will be about thirty minutes.

Keep him busy. Like, what am I supposed to do? What if he wants to go out and get some food? What if he wants to.... OMG!

I message Emily that the police are on their way.

I go up the elevator—at least they have an elevator. I find the room and knock. Chase opens the door, grabs me in a bear hug, and swings me around. The scarf flies off my neck onto the floor.

"I got a couple of other video commercials because they loved you in the rowing video. I worked with one of their models, and we nailed it. My site is going viral, and it's all because of you. I'm sorry it took me so long. I had to do some editing and set up some contracts. That town is very serious about its water sports."

I bet you did have to do some editing.

I turn so he can't see my face. He'll see right through me. "Let me drop this pack," I say, and go over to a low counter and put it down. He closes the door behind me, and I jump when it clicks shut. Sitting on the desk chair, I start taking off my shoes.

"You look like you're in pain. What's up?"

"I think the thirty klicks over the mountain did my foot in."

He kneels in front of me and examines my foot. "Yep, you have a big blister on the bottom of your foot. Let me fix it." He rummages for his first aid kit in his pack.

I'm going to turn this man in to the police, and he wants to fix my foot. I'm such a Judas.

He cleans the needle and thread with an alcohol pad,

punctures the blister, and draws the thread through it. He cuts the thread and leaves it in the blister to drain. Then he puts a bandage over it.

That's amazing. It feels so much better.

He kisses my foot. "Better?"

My eyes well up with tears. "Yes, better. We need to talk."

"I know you think I ghosted you, but I did it for us. I made enough to pay for a few nights in this hotel with some leftover." He grins. "You'll need to rest a couple of days for your foot to heal. We'll take a vacation from our vacation. You must be hungry. Why don't you take a shower, change, and then we'll go out for a nice meal. We can talk over tapas."

"All right." My phone dings. A message from the policeman: *We're on our way up.*

I rummage in my pack for my clean clothes and toiletries, taking more time than I need. I hide my face so he can't see what I'm thinking.

A knock, and I rush to the door.

The policeman walks in, deliberately putting himself in front of me.

"Are you Chase Damon?" he asks.

"Why do you want to know?"

"May I see some ID?"

Chase pulls out his passport and shows it to the policeman. He's playing it cool.

"What's going on?" Chase looks at me, then at the policeman, then back to me. "Do you know anything about this?"

Blood rushes to my face. "I told them about the videos and PornNow."

"PornNow, what's that?" He says it so innocently.

Am I wrong? Maybe he didn't do it. I step up beside the policeman, closer to Chase. I look into his eyes. Is he telling the truth?

The policeman tells him that he is being arrested for posting nude videos of me for money without my permission. Then he reads him his rights.

Chase's face turns red. "You bitch." He lunges for me, steps on the scarf, and slips, falling to his knees. "I'm not going to hurt you. I love you. I'm making us money and you turn me in. You wanted it too."

"I was all right with helping you make videos for the YouTube channel, but not in the nude. I've never stripped in front of you."

Getting to his feet, his lips tighten and curl inward. He points his finger in my face. "Well, close enough in that skimpy suit, showing off your body. There's no law against posting pictures of you in a swimsuit, especially when you agreed to it."

"Yes, I agreed to the videos of me in a swimsuit, but not to the nude ones." Anger has replaced my shame.

"But I didn't post any videos of you nude on YouTube," he says, raising his palms and shrugging. His eyes dart nervously past the policeman to the door.

"Sir, may I remind you of your rights? Miss James, do you stand by your accusation?"

I look at Chase and the policeman. If I say yes, Chase goes to jail. If I say no, will he forgive me? Is it a misunderstanding?

The scarf is on the floor where it tripped Chase. I think of Emily. My phone dings. A text from Emily: *Stand strong.*

She went to bat for me. I can't let her down.

"Y-yes, sir, I do. There are nude pictures of me on PornNow, and I never posed for them. They were photoshopped without my permission."

The policeman turns back to Chase. "Sir, you are under arrest."

"I'm an American citizen. You can't arrest me."

"Yes, sir, I can. And I want to remind you again that anything you say will and can be used against you."

Chase explodes and grabs me. "You cunt. You wanted it. I could tell." He draws his hand back to slap me. The policeman grabs his arm and bends it behind his back, then grabs the other arm and cuffs him.

"Sir, I am adding attempted assault to the charges."

"I'm getting a lawyer. I need to make some phone calls."

"We can discuss this when we get to the police station," he tells him. Then he looks at me. "Are you all right?"

"Yes, sir, I'm fine. Just shaking."

"Call me and keep me informed of your whereabouts. We're going to need an official statement."

"Yes, sir."

He takes Chase out the door. I grab Chase's pack and carry it down to the waiting vehicle. They leave, and I walk back into the hotel and lean against the wall.

"Are you all right?" the desk clerk asks me.

"Yes, sir. I am. Gracias." I take the elevator back up to our room.

I can't stay here. I begin packing and pick up the scarf from the floor, smooth it out, and put it around my neck. With one last look around the room, I go back downstairs to the desk. "I can't stay here," I tell the receptionist.

"Well, Miss, there are no refunds, and you must pay for the night whether you stay or not."

"What? I thought Chase had paid for the room."

"Well, he held it with a credit card. You are Valerie James, and this is your credit card number, isn't it?"

"But I didn't make the reservation. Chase did."

"This is your card, is it not?"

"Well, yes. Just put me in a different room."

"No problem."

I get a new key and head back upstairs. There's a message from Emily to call her. I tell her about the arrest and that Chase was even going to stick me with the credit card bill. He must have gotten my card number, which I gave him to pay for the e-SIM at the airport and lunch in Irún. I haven't checked my credit card statement since I arrived. What an idiot.

Emily helps me think through everything. We hang up, and I check my statement. There are charges for food and a hotel in Ribadesella. He was living it up on my dime. I call the credit card company to let them know what happened. They cancel my card and tell me a new one will be mailed to me.

"I'm in Spain," I tell the representative. "Where are they going to send it? I need it now. How will I live the next few weeks?"

She tells me they can overnight it to the hotel where I'm staying. Of course. It probably happens all the time.

I call the front desk and explain about the card and how they're sending me a new one. They offer to rent me a room for a second night while I wait for my card to arrive.

OMG. Why did I fall for his lies? Why didn't I just stick with my original plan to go to Sarria, walk to Santiago, and fly home? I'm such a loser. I will be in so much debt and can't ask Mom for help. This mess is on me. She wasn't happy with me going in the first place, much less me changing my plans for a man.

I get in the shower. Looking at my foot, I remember how tenderly he treated it. All the evidence points to his guilt, but he can also be so nice and kind. I don't understand. I slip into bed, exhausted, but I just can't turn my brain off.

. . .

I must have slept. Now awake and hungry, I go out to a cafe and spend five of my last fifty euros on coffee and a tortilla. A message from the policeman asks me to come to the station to give a statement. When I get there, I ask if I can see Chase. The policeman says yes, but only after I give my statement. I give him my statement, and he takes me to the visiting room. Chase is on the other side of a glass wall, and it looks like his night was as bad as mine.

"I'm sorry," he says. "How's your foot?"

"It's much better. Thank you for fixing it. Why did you use my credit card?"

"I was going to pay you back when I got paid. The money from the ad and my YouTube channel are being deposited tomorrow. I didn't think you would mind. We're a team."

"But you should have asked."

"Yes, I know. And I'm really sorry. I didn't think you would mind. We're so good together."

My resolve is crumbling. What did I do to make him think we had that kind of relationship?

"Look, Chase, I'm sorry you thought that I would agree with you, but you should have asked. You don't know anything about my card or my bills."

"Well, I figured you would forgive me when I paid you back and more than what I owed you. I had such great plans for us here in Gijón. It's an awesome city. I know you love plants, and I was going to take you to the botanical gardens, but you messed that all up." His tone changes. "You couldn't wait to talk to me. You had to call the police. I could have straightened it out. You don't understand."

"Well, why don't you explain it?" I'm getting testy.

"Too late. You jumped to conclusions, and now I have to pay for it. Your word against mine, and women always get a break. You just have to bat those eyelashes, and they believe you."

"Tell me what I got wrong," I say.

"Too late. Just leave me alone. I never want to see you again."

"But Chase, if I misunderstood, please set me straight."

"You don't care about me." He calls the guard and is taken back to his cell.

I feel like a louse. Did I really misunderstand? Maybe

he's telling the truth, and the rowing shop guy did it. That guy was leering at me.

I call Emily. She reminds me that some people, for whatever reason, simply cannot tell the truth. She states that whether he lied or not is for the courts to decide. She tells me that she contacted a friend who is an online content compliance officer at one of the companies she works with. He does extensive cybersecurity, and they have a contingency for this kind of crime. Because I made a police report, they can hide the video of me from the public. A copy will be kept for evidence. She just needs a copy of the report.

I pull the report out of my backpack, take a picture and send it to her. "Please ask them to hide it."

"I already did. I'll forward the report. I assumed you would want that."

"Thank you so much. It's amazing that I met you when I needed you most."

She smiles, "What are your plans?"

"Tomorrow, I walk to Avilés."

"Good on you. One day at a time. This Camino is about you. Stay in touch, and I'll let you know if I learn anything."

As I walk back to the hotel, I bump into the two ladies I had dinner with last night in Villaviciosa.

"Valerie, we just walked in from Peón. We stayed in the most delightful little farmhouse. When did you get in?"

"I walked in yesterday from Villaviciosa. Are you staying at this hotel?"

"Yes, and you? I thought you stayed at albergues."

"I'm here tonight. It's a long story."

"Well, why don't you tell us over dinner? I'm exhausted and want a shower. Let's meet down here at seven p.m.."

"Sounds good," I give them my WhatsApp number, go to my room, and collapse on the bed. I'm exhausted, but I can't stay still. I go to the lobby and ask the receptionist what I should see while I'm here. He pulls out a tourist map and points to the old part of the town. I take the map and walk to the marina in front of the hotel, then follow the road as it climbs to the old town. The streets are narrow, and there's some graffiti. It's not as pristine as some of the other ancient towns I've seen.

I aimlessly wander the streets. A plaque on a stone facade gets my attention. It's the only thing distinguishing it from the abutting buildings. 'Capilla de Nuestra Señora de los Remedios.' The plaque says that the chapel is a place for spiritual healing, linked to a hospital founded in the fifteenth century to care for sick pilgrims.

The door is open, and I go in. The chapel is very simple, with a statue of the Virgin Mary in a niche behind the altar. I slide into one of the pews and bow my head. My mind is blank as I sit in meditation. I don't know what to pray for.

I succumb to the numbness of my mind.

A group of tourists comes in whispering, but sometimes whispers can be louder than yelling. I give thanks, slide out of the pew, genuflect, and cross myself. The tourists nod at me, and I nod back as I brush past them to the back of the chapel. Stopping at the donation box, I slip in a euro and light a candle. I make my way back to the hotel, feeling more at peace.

My phone rings as I walk into my room. It's Helen.

"You sound tired," she says when I pick up. "Tell me what's going on."

I vomit out the whole story. "I was kidding myself that I could do this. It's a disaster. I'm coming home."

"Now that I have heard the bad things that have happened to you, and I don't want to minimize these, I, too, had some very difficult moments on my Camino. What are the blessings you have received?"

"Blessings?" I can't think of any. My savings are gone. I've been abused by someone I trusted. My heart is just not up for it. Blessings? Who is she kidding?

"How's your heart, physically? How's your breathing?"

"You are such the nurse." I do a quick check, "Actually, I am really good. Only the steepest grades speed up my heart and breathing, but I recover really fast. And that happens to everyone. It's emotionally where things are breaking down."

"You are about two-thirds into your Camino. This is about the time things have broken down emotionally. There is a saying about the Camino that the first part is physical, the second is emotional, and the third is integration. I believe you owe it to yourself to integrate everything you are learning."

A sob comes bursting out of me. "It's too hard."

"Do you have support?"

"Well, I have you, and now Emily. I met three fantastic siblings and a dog. I'm having dinner tonight with two ladies I met in Villaviciosa."

"Give it a few more days. Chase will not be in your space. You can take the time to sort things out. You call me anytime. We nurses have to stick together. Where's your next stop?"

"I haven't even looked."

"I'm looking at a map right now and see the town of Avilés. Call me when you get in." Helen's voice is pure kindness.

"Ok, I will. And thank you."

"You are very welcome, Valerie. I'm so proud of you," she says, and we hang up.

A warm light flows through my body. I take the scarf and hug it, then head out for dinner.

The ladies I met in Villaviciosa and I return from dinner. We make arrangements to meet the next morning to take the bus to Avilés. They tell me that their guidebook recommends this because it's an industrial area almost all the way. Now exhausted, I go to my room and fall into bed.

. . .

I wake up feeling better than I have in ages. I get my new credit card from the front desk and meet the ladies for breakfast. We then walk to the bus station.

The twenty-five kilometers fly by on the bus, and we are let off at the station in Avilés. I say goodbye to my new friends and walk to the only albergue in town. There's a sign on the door: 'Closed for repairs.' At least my translate app is working. There are only hotels, and I can't afford that. I spot a yellow arrow and keep moving forward.

The path takes me through the city and then a residential area. I finally break free of the city, and an arrow points to a dirt path through the woods. My guidebook says it's a shortcut that avoids the main road and enters the town of Salinas.

The book shows a donative albergue at the top of a hill just outside of town. I check the map and the app. They align. I get back on the road and find an arrow that points up a curving road. Some things never change. It's always uphill.

Digging in, I reach the small albergue at the top of the hill. It's flanked by a church. The Dorans are sitting out front, watching Maeloc romp in the grass. His head comes up. He sniffs the wind, turns, and races to me as I enter the long driveway to the albergue. Brigit yells for him to come back.

I yell her name. She smiles and comes running down the drive to meet me. She grabs me and hugs me.

OMG, Helen was so right. If I had given up, I never would have seen these friends again.

The boys join us, and Lugh takes my pack for the last couple of yards to the front door. The hospitalera assigns me a bunk in their room. I shower and wash my dirty clothes.

I'm hanging them on the line when the hospitalera asks if I can help set the table for dinner. I follow her in, and she shows me where to get everything. I fold the napkins into cute little hats for each place, then go out and pick some wildflowers. She gives me a couple of water glasses to make flower arrangements for the table. It looks beautiful.

There are about thirty of us for dinner, which includes vegetable stew, bread, and flan for dessert. Of course, wine is the other national food group. The laughter and stories ring in all languages. After we finish eating, one of the pilgrims pulls out a guitar and starts to play. He sings a song that most of the pilgrims seem to know: Ultreia, and it's in French. I hum along to the chorus.

"What does Ultreia mean?" I ask Brigit.

"Onward, keep going."

The pilgrim then begins a guitar solo, and Brigit pulls me up to dance.

"It's the Malagueña," she exclaims.

Everyone claps to the beat to encourage us. The music becomes faster, and I pretend I'm a flamenco dancer. I stomp my feet and whirl around the room. Brigit and I put on quite a breathless performance. The music ends and we bow to the crowd. The hospitalero whispers something to the guitarist, and he puts his instrument away. She gathers us for a prayer then sends us to bed. We have an early day, and a long thirty-two-kilometer walk tomorrow.

CHAPTER 13

SAN MARTÍN DE LESPRA TO MONDOÑERO

We hit the road this morning, and it has been almost all road-walking to get us to the next little donativo. We called yesterday to ensure they would take us and Maeloc. If we choose to take the optional route over the mountain, the owner suggests we stop at a market on the way into town to buy lunch for tomorrow. There will not be any facilities once we leave the donativo, but I hear the views are spectacular.

We arrive at the small farmhouse on the outskirts of Martín de Laspra. The owner shows us our bunks and where to put our dirty clothes. If we drop them in the basket by five p.m., she will wash them all. Her husband prepares a delicious stew with fresh vegetables from their garden. I caught him slipping Maeloc a bone.

I text Helen, Emily, and Mom to let them know I am back on my way and walking with the Doran family. I also text the police, so they know where I am. There wasn't enough signal to do anything else.

. . .

I wake up refreshed. Stepping outside, I see the early rays of the sun peeking through the trees. The weather promises to be good, so we decide to take the high road over the mountain. We eat breakfast, and the owner makes sure all our water containers are full. I just can't get over how well the Spanish care for us.

The arrows point us through small hamlets and fields with cows, goats, and crops. We are back in the country. I feel like I can breathe. The path turns upward, and we climb the mountain.

We quickly reach the top. My breath has been good, and my heart is strong. Intention accomplished. Pausing at the top of the mountain, I take in the spectacular view of the countryside. It's so good to be out here walking.

The view from the top of the mountain reminds me that all things up close look big but then become insignificant as we gain a greater perspective. I'm also grateful to be with the siblings and Maeloc. I'm so grateful for both Emily and Helen. I feel safe.

Cú stops to sit with me. Brigit and Lugh keep walking with Maeloc.

"I checked the website, and the video of you is gone."

"Oh, thank God. I didn't have the courage to look."

"I-I'm ashamed to admit that I've spent time on those kinds of websites. I guess it's a guy thing. But I never thought about it being real girls with families and lives, girls who may not even know that an innocent video of them has been shopped to make it into entertainment for men."

"Yeah, sometimes we forget the people online are real people with feelings and lives. It's scary."

"I'm never going to look at one of those sites again," he says vehemently. "I wouldn't want people looking at me."

"Thank you. That means so much." I smile at him. "Vamos."

"Vamos," he echoes, and we start walking.

The slope back down the mountain is steep and slippery. We take our time, treading carefully. We arrive in the town of Cadavedo and find a place to stay. Once again, Maeloc is made to stay outside on his leash.

. . .

The days have melted into each other as we continue west along the coast. The Camino veers inland again to Otur. We stop at a small home with fourteen beds for pilgrims. It has an open field to the back and is flanked by houses on either side.

The owner, Mercedes, is a nurse and opens her home to pilgrims when she's not working at the hospital. She asks us to remove our packs and shoes outside and place them in plastic bags in a lockable storage bin beside the house. We can only bring in our change of clothes and toiletries. She doesn't want anyone to inadvertently bring bedbugs into her home.

Now clean, I enter the main room, which serves as a kitchen, dining room, and living room. There is a small, cozy area with a wood-burning fireplace. The smell of a vegetable stew comes from the stove. Mercedes is at the small stove, fixing our meal. She does this for donations. There are no guarantees that pilgrims will want to stop and stay or even donate. She is so trusting.

I offer to help, and she assigns me to setting the long wooden table. This is becoming my Camino job. I finish and wander to the couch. A colorful book on the coffee table catches my eye. I flip through it. It's written in three languages. Mercedes tells me that it is a guide to a tarot deck written and illustrated by her friend, who also owns a donativo outside of Mondoñedo in Maariz.

The illustrations are done in bold colors and look quite mystical. I ask about the languages, and she tells me it's written in Spanish, Galician, and English.

"Galician?"

"Yes, at one time, each of these provinces was a small country unto themselves. Before motor travel, these areas were isolated and had self-rule. With the advent of a more mobile society, Spain has melded into one country, but each area still holds onto its roots. It's even encouraged. We must honor our roots to move forward."

"What province are we in now?"

"You are in Asturias."

"Oh yeah, Emily told me that. I'm becoming quite fond of Asturias."

"We were once the capital of Spain. Oviedo is still the capital of Asturias. Do you know the story of how St. James' relic was discovered?"

"No, actually I don't. I know he's buried in Santiago, but I never thought much about how that happened."

"St. James, the Greater, was one of the original twelve Apostles of Jesus. After Jesus was crucified, James was sent to Spain to evangelize and bring the pagans to Christianity. He didn't feel he was doing a very good job and returned to Jerusalem to admit defeat to the other apostles. When he arrived, he too, was betrayed, and King Herod Agrippa had him beheaded.

"Two of James' disciples put his remains in a stone boat and brought him back to Spain, where his remains were placed in a cave. In the ninth century, a farmer saw a light in the forest and went to investigate. He found a cave containing old bones. He went immediately to inform his parish priest. The priest went to Bishop Theodemir, who went to the King of Spain, Alfonso II, in Oviedo, Asturias. Alfonso II and his wife, Queen Berta, made the long trek of over three hundred kilometers to the cave and determined that these bones were the relics of St. James. The king ordered a small chapel to be built to honor St. James on the spot. James was more successful than he believed."

"Is that the Primitivo Route?"

"Yes, Primitivo means first. It was the first pilgrimage route to Santiago. Word spread of this chapel and the miracles people experienced when they arrived. The area was soon overrun with pilgrims. King Alfonso II and Queen Berta made a second pilgrimage to the area and authorized the building of a cathedral. When you arrive in Santiago, you'll be immersed in the rich history of the shrine and city, spanning thousands of years.

"So, with all of this Christianity, why am I running into pagans, witches and tarot cards?" I ask.

"We are a people who have learned to co-exist. We can keep the ancient beliefs, festivals, and rituals of our roots and incorporate the newer beliefs of Christianity.

We find that we are much richer by embracing our complete past."

"New is definitely relative. I think of Christianity as old," I tell her.

"Yes, in a culture such as ours, Christianity is new. If you choose to stop in Maariz and learn more about the tarot, I will phone Katova and let her know you are coming."

"Thank you."

"Now, please let everyone know dinner is served."

. . .

Another really good night's sleep. I am learning that I can sleep anywhere. This is a great skill for a nurse. We begin to repack on the porch. Mercedes comes out and suggests we try an alternative way to take us back to the sea. I look at the siblings, and they are in agreement.

The directions she provided are easy to follow, and we wind our way down through a forest to a small, deserted beach— much like the place where I first met them.

Maeloc goes off to frolic in the surf as we make a greeting for pilgrims in the sand with shells. Just as our hospitalero described, the beach ends at a small stream with a rocky bed. We remove our shoes and socks and ford through the cold water running off from the mountains.

I sit on a rock on the other side of the stream and let the sun soak into my body. I eat a snack to boost my energy for climbing the wooden staircase clinging to the side of the bluff. The warm air quickly dries my feet. The thread has fallen out of the blister, and it has become a protective callus.

I reflect on all that has transpired since I left home. Home seems like a distant place. This is my reality now. Mercedes sounded so positive about me walking into Santiago. I still have about two hundred fifty kilometers to go. I better get started.

The Dorans have finished their snacks and are putting on their shoes too. Cú looks at me and says, "Vamos."

The kilometers and towns melt away beneath our feet. Steep inclines become child's play as my body becomes trail-hardened. The Camino meanders along the bluffs by the sea and then takes us inland through mountain passes. Whoever laid this out was a genius. It probably wasn't just one person, but a community dedicated to pilgrims and themselves. They want the Camino to pass through their village, bringing commerce. There are many compromises and choices to consider.

I look back at my choices, knowing they're the reason I'm here—through the good and the bad. I wonder what is happening to Chase.

. . .

The terrain begins to change, and the Camino becomes a bit flatter. The Dorans and I fall into a rhythm. Sometimes, we stay together, and sometimes, they go off on their own. It's weird how walking is like a way of life. When there's an option, we choose the Costal Senda path, preferring the sea, bluffs, and beaches to the mountains.

We once again turn inland to the town of Figueras. It's a bustling metropolis. There are nice suburban homes in well-laid-out neighborhoods. Almost all the houses have walls or fences covered in roses. The fragrance is intoxicating.

We pass a yard where the owner has decorated it to look like the land of the hobbits. There are little statues of dwarves peeking out from the multicolored hydrangea. The bushes are trimmed to look like turtles, miniature spiral trees, and mushrooms. There's a bench overlooking a small water feature, and a cat is sleeping on it in the sun. I'd join the cat in an afternoon nap

The sidewalk leads us to a market in the city center. I stop at a stall selling clothes. They remind me of the clothes my mom wore in the 1970s: cheesecloth, flowing pants, and skirts with embroidery and tassels. A pair of pants calls my name. I know if I buy them, I'll have to carry them, but they're so cute. The stall owner directs me to a curtain enclosure to try them on.

There's a mirror hanging from an overhead pipe. Oh, I'm sunk now. I love them. I feel so pretty. It's been a long time since I have worn something pretty. I'm so tired of the same two outfits.

"They're perfect on you," the proprietor says, encouraging the sale. She gives me a good price. I just can't walk away from them. I change back into my shorts and pay her. I roll up the pants and shove them into my pack. I know I'll have the opportunity to wear them.

I continue my stroll through the market, where there's a man with a table full of wonderful fruit. The cherries are a deep red and incredibly shiny. They seem to say, "Eat me." I stop and ask for a handful. He places a bunch in a bag and waves me off when I reach for my coin purse. Not quite understanding, I open my purse.

He shakes his head and says, "*Para peregrina.*"

"For me, a pilgrim, for free?"

"Sí," he says. "Buen Camino."

I'm so overcome. This man just gave me food because I'm a pilgrim.

I catch up with the siblings, and we go to a park at the river's edge. The river is the boundary between the provinces of Asturias and Galicia. We find a bench and share food. The cherries are delicious.

We make our way to the bridge that spans the Ribadeo

River and takes us into Galicia. It's the longest bridge I have ever walked across. The water seems so far below. I can see it through the metal grate of the pedestrian catwalk. I look up, trying to find something less terrifying to look at.

I look straight ahead at the traffic and see a truck barreling down the road toward me. Not a good call. There's only a short chain-link fence separating me from the truck. It wouldn't withstand a collision. The entire bridge shakes.

"Breathe," Lugh tells me.

"I didn't realize I was holding my breath."

"It's scary, but holding your breath is not the answer."

"You're right. I just have to keep moving forward, and we'll get to the other side."

He smiles. "Ultreia, that's the trick."

We safely get to the other side and make our way into town. The marina and hotels are at the edge of the river. The old, main part of town is above it on a bluff. There is even an elevator to get between the two. I opt for the albergue up in the old town. The Dorans will find a place to camp outside of town.

I sign in right behind a group of pilgrims from France. I stake out a bunk, shower, and wash my clothes. It's still early, and the other pilgrims are talking about a cathedral. I walk over and ask about the cathedral. I would like to go to mass.

"*Ce n'est pas une église*," one of the women say.

"Not a church?" I query, hoping I understood what she said.

Her friend, who speaks English, chimes in. "No, it's not a church. It's a place where the sea has carved fantastic formations out of the rocks. You must join us. We leave in one hour. It will be low tide."

"Thank you, I'd love to join you."

I quickly scan my email, texts, and Facebook, and I also check in with the police. There's no news, but there's a text from Emilia: *I haven't been compromised. Thank you for your concern. I told you he was possessed.*

I walk to the front of the albergue and join the group from France. It's two couples and two friends who are walking together. We go to the tourist information center on the square and buy tickets for the bus to take us to Cathedral Beach. The driver says we will have two hours on the beach before the next bus comes to take us back to town.

The bus lets us out on the side of the road, and we walk towards a touristy-looking building with a cafe. There are loads of people having a meal. A walkway leads to a staircase beside a waterfall that takes us down to the beach. The tide is still going out and uncovering the entrance to caves in the rocks. I make my way along the beach, climbing over rocks and wading through shallow pools. I come upon a cave and enter the semi-darkness. The tunnel bends to the left. A bit of light flickers ahead and I continue to explore. The sound of crashing waves is amplified through the rock. A person could get lost in here.

I step into a chamber and the light is coming in from above. I'm at the bottom of a blowhole. It's amazing. The only way out is the way I came in. I wouldn't want to get caught in here when the tide comes in.

I exit the cave and cross the beach to a large rocky structure emerging from the surf. At high tide, the top would only be visible as an offshore rock, but the entrance becomes more evident as the tide recedes.

I believe the water is shallow enough, so I time the waves and go into the rock. The center is hollow and full of sand and shells. A delicate pink shell captures my attention. How could it survive in such a harsh environment? I squat down to pick up the shell. A wave rushes through the opening in the rock and knocks me flat on my butt, and washes over me, leaving a deposit of sand. I sit up and take the scarf from around my neck. I rinse it in the pool of water next to me and use it to wipe off the sand. The next few waves don't make it as far into the chamber.

I lean back and gaze at the ceiling, a masterpiece sculpted by the sea over millennia. The carved shapes form a shifting collage, and my imagination brings them to life—a horse and a woman etched into the rock. I picture them galloping along the shore, the wind streaming through her hair and lifting the horse's tail. A man with a spear runs beside her, their movements filled with pure joy and unrestrained freedom.

The next wave comes in, washes more sand from my body, and my vision changes. It looks like rows of beds— it could be a ward in a hospital or an albergue. I laugh at the thought. Another wave, and the picture changes to a village. I feel at home in this ancient village. Another huge wave rushes in and covers me.

"Valerie," a woman calls to me.

I sit up and shake off the water. Just like Maeloc. I laugh and go to the entrance of the chamber. "Over here."

She looks me over, concerned. I pantomime being knocked down by a wave, laughing at my clumsiness. This reassures her, and she joins me in laughter.

"Oh, I was so worried. I could not find you, and the bus will be here soon. We must go."

"Thank you," I say as I walk into the surf to rid myself of the rest of the sand. I use the scarf to scrub it off and remove some of the water. We make our way across the sand. I continue to drip dry.

I'm lost in the visions I saw in the cave, but the French woman's voice pulls me back to the present. She asks me to join them for dinner and I agree. We arrive back in town and make our way to the albergue. I shower and put on my half-dry clothes that have been hanging on the line. I wash the salty sandy ones and hang them out to dry. That's one disadvantage to having only two sets of clothes. But, suddenly remember, I have new pants and am meeting the French for dinner. I must look stylish. Pulling on my new pants with my half-dry top, I look at myself in the mirror. Cute!

We have a lovely meal and head back to the albergue. I fall into bed and call my mom. She picks up on the first ring.

"Have you ever been to Kenya, where Dad grew up?" I ask.

"No. It was so far away, and we never had the money or the time. Why?"

"I was thinking about our ancestors today and wondered. Have you ever wanted to go?"

"When we first married, I was really interested, but the demands of our lives never allowed it. Time just got away from us, and then your father died. Are you interested in going?"

"I think so. I know now is not the time, and I don't have the money, especially after this trip. But one day."

"Let's talk when you get home," she says. The phone goes quiet for a minute. "Sorry, I have a friend visiting." Another hesitation, then she adds, "You sound good."

"I am good." I realize this is true as I say it. "Talk soon. Love you, Mom."

"Love you too."

I turn over and close my eyes

. . .

I wake up ravenous and go to find breakfast before I start walking.

The Camino leads out of town and up a mountain. I've seen the last of the Cantabrian sea. I'm going to climb the Galician plateau to Santiago.

The landscape morphs into fields and forests. The towns are few and far between. I stop at a bridge over a river with a freshwater fountain of potable water. And a bench for tired pilgrims to sit and rest. There's a farmhouse just up a driveway running by the stream. A woman comes out with a fresh buttered roll with cheese and ham for me.

She refuses my offer to pay, looks me directly in the eye, and says, "Pray for me in Santiago. My name is Agatha. " She waves her hand in front of her chest. I see that her top is baggy where there should be breasts.

I take her hands and smile at her, letting her know that I will keep her in my prayers. She smiles, turns, and makes her way back to her small home.

I will pray for her. Agatha. I repeat her name, so I remember it. I take a moment to express gratitude for the food and this generous woman. I bite into the sandwich, and the flavors dissolve in my mouth. It's delicious—better than the stale nuts and tangerine on my backpack.

It starts to drizzle, so I don my poncho. I begin to walk, and the wind becomes colder and stronger as I gain elevation. The rain starts pouring down in torrents which, strangely enough, makes me laugh. I simply can't seem to stay dry, and just when I think it can't get any worse, it does. The sky opens up with thunder and lightning. It's raining so hard that I can hardly see where I'm going. There is no place to take shelter. I lean into the wind and feel like I am making very little progress. But I can't stop. Ultreia. I start humming the song. It gives me courage.

I come to a crossroads where there are a few buildings. The arrows appear out of the storm and indicate a left-hand turn. I turn left. There's a sign for a cafe and hotel out here in the middle of nowhere. I stop and step into the door of the cafe. It's bright and warm. The smell of freshly baked bread is tantalizing.

The proprietor comes out from behind the counter and assists me in removing my poncho. She hangs it on a stand in the corner over a coat rack to dry. There's a shelf on the wall full of Camino souvenirs.

I take a deep breath and say, "Gracias." I pull the scarf from around my neck to dry off my face. It's come in handy for many things.

She asks in wonderful English if I would like a bed for the night. I can tell that this place won't fit my budget, but I can't face going back out in the rain. I have never racked up such a large bill on my credit card before. I hope I have some credit left.

Thoughts of a warm, dry bed win out over debt. I hand her my credit card. 'Approved' pops up in the machine's window. I sigh in relief. She calls her husband, who comes with a large umbrella and leads me across the yard to a modern hotel. He tells me that dinner will be served at seven p.m. on the third floor.

I jump into a hot shower and let the water warm my chilled body. I get out and wash my clothes in the sink in my bathroom. My own bathroom. What a gift. I notice that the towel rack has a knob on the side. I have never seen one like this. It dawns on me that it's hooked up to the radiator and I can turn it on. I turn up the heat and hang my wet clothes on it to dry. I take a picture of the towel rack and post it on Instagram, with the caption: Warm and dry in Spain.

A glance at my watch tells me I have time to nap before dinner. I set the alarm and cozy under the covers. The last of the chill disappears.

I head upstairs for dinner. The French group greets me as I enter the dining room. The proprietor comes in with a huge paella containing mussels, fish, sausage, ham, veggies, and everything else. The paella is accompanied by wine, salad, bread, and dessert. There's so much food, and I eat more than my share. The French do a good job keeping up with me.

I'm so glad one of the ladies speaks English. How lame am I? I only speak one language.

The French consume an extraordinary amount of wine, and I do my best to keep up. I don't need to drive; I can walk downstairs to my room. During dessert, the proprietor informs us that breakfast is self-serve in the kitchen and will be available starting at six a.m.

. . .

The sun is rising as I make my way to the kitchen for coffee. It will be just the thing to shake off the fog of the hangover. One of the patrons has the coffee going and toast in the oven.

"Bless you." I reach for a cup and help myself to orange juice. Here in Spain, the juice is fresh squeezed, and I love it. I pick up an apple and put some cheese in a baggie for my lunch.

Over toast and coffee, we look at our guides. The group from France is headed to Mondoñedo. It is one of the largest towns in this area, with a cathedral on which construction started in 1219. The church has gone through many changes from Romanesque to Gothic to Baroque. It is known as the Catedral Arrodillada, which translates to Kneeling Cathedral because of its perfect proportions for its short stature. It also has an ancient rose window.

"What's a 'rose window?'" I ask.

"You've seen them," the French woman explains. "It is the term for a circular window with decorative supports through it, usually of stone and in-between stained glass."

"Yeah, I know exactly what you are talking about. I've seen them in many of the churches. They're beautiful."

"The rose window is a magnificent example of the intersection of art and architecture. It's a symbol of unity and wholeness. The parts are perfectly balanced. There are five important components to a rose window: light, circle, cycle, order, and geometry. It's a bit metaphysical within a sacred space. I believe these concepts could be one and the same, with just a different name."

"Did you just read that, or do you know it?" I ask.

She smiles at me. "I make a study of these churches."

"May I join you for a tour of the cathedral when we arrive?"

"Of course. And you must also join us to see the Sanctuary of Remedios and the Hospital of San Pablo, both built in the sixteenth century."

A Sanctuary of Remedies. I recall sitting in the sanctuary in Gijón and peace floods my body.

I look at the guidebook and realize once I reach Mondoñedo, I only have three more kilometers to walk to the donativo where the lady who made the tarot deck lives. I call her and confirm that I'll be there later in the afternoon. She tells me that she will have a vegetarian dinner waiting for me.

CHAPTER 14

MONDOÑERO TO PARGA

The Way out of Mondoñedo is an uphill dirt path between fields. Of course, it is. The path empties me out onto an asphalt road that goes through a forest with very few houses. I wonder how Maeloc's feet are doing. It seems we are walking more on asphalt now than on dirt paths.

A sign at the end of a driveway reads 'O Bisonte,' and it has a red buffalo painted on it. It leads to a stone farmhouse. Oh, it must be a bison, not a buffalo. Sometimes, I'm so lame.

A dog barks, and I see Maeloc running towards me. I crouch down and hug his neck. He about licks me to death. The Dorans are close on his heels.

"We're together again," Brigit says, and as I stand, she hugs me. "Come meet Katova. She and our mom are great friends."

We all link arms and walk to a picnic table covered by a makeshift roof. Katova comes out and greets me.

She gets right to business and tells me to put my pack and everything I don't need for the night in a plastic box. My change of clothes and toiletries can come into the house with me. She points to a cubby by the door where I am to leave my dirty shoes. I slip on my sandals and enter the home.

There's a washing machine by the front door. On the other side there's an open door behind which is a staircase leading up to the rooms. I bet she closes it in the winter to conserve heat. In front of me there is a hallway with a dining room poking out from behind a door. A door to my immediate left beside the washing machine leads into the kitchen. The whole place looks to be made of ancient stone.

Katova orients me to my room upstairs, then takes me to the bathroom accessed outside and around the back of the house. It, too, is made of stone. She says that the canvas paintings on the walls are her work. They are of bold colors with reclining figures. In the places where the walls are covered in stucco, there are paintings with ancient motifs, handprints, horses, and bison. The shower has no curtain and is just part of the stonework with two steps leading up to it. There's also a couch and a desk in the large room where you can relax after a shower. This is the most amazing bathroom I have ever seen. I could spend hours in here just looking at the artwork.

But I quickly shower and dress. When I return to the front door, Katova takes my dirty clothes and throws them in the washing machine with those of the Dorans. She invites me into her small kitchen where she offers me a cup of tea made from the herbs in her garden. I feel welcome.

Brigit pops her head into the kitchen, "You've got to see the art studio."

Katova smiles and takes my empty cup. We walk across the yard to what I thought was an old barn and go up some steps into an open room with easels, paints, tables, and chairs. There on a long table is her tarot book, just like the one I saw at Mercedes' donativo in Otur, with a deck of matching cards next to it.

I walk over to the book and leaf through it. "It's beautiful." I pick up a deck of cards. The back has a sacred spiral, and each card is painted in the same bold colors as the paintings in the bathroom.

"This was my COVID project," Katova says. "I had been inspired to make a tarot deck with Galician lore for many years, but COVID gave me the quiet and the time to complete the project."

"Your English is wonderful," I observe.

"I spent several years working in America. That's where I learned to speak English."

"Do you give people readings?"

"Only if they are open, and it feels right to me." She cocks her head like she's listening to someone who is whispering in her ear. "I can do a reading for you if you wish."

"I would love that."

"Do you want your friends here or not?" she asks.

She must be is trying to respect my privacy. I look over at Lugh who is in a chair, stroking a very content cat sitting on his lap. Cú says he wants to take Maeloc for a walk before dark and leaves. Brigit is engrossed in creating her own artwork. It's fine that they are here. There are no secrets.

Katova lights a piece of holly and asks me to stretch out my arms. Then she takes the smoking piece of wood and smudges me with it. She motions for me to join her at a small round table covered with a beautiful cloth. After lighting a candle, she becomes quiet.

Next, she hands me the deck of cards and instructs me to mix them up and cut them with my left hand while I think about my intention for the reading. I ask for clarity and light to show me what I need to know. I place the cards on my right as instructed. The situation with Chase is at the forefront of my mind.

She asks me to give her a card from the top of the deck using my left hand. I do this five more times as she places them in what she calls the 'pentagram spread' on the table.

"The first card is your current situation. It is 'Os Loboshomes,' the werewolf." She looks at me with concern. "There is a man, a partner in your life, that is creating great danger for you."

I gasp. Oh shit. Chase. I look at Brigit. "Did you tell her about me?"

"No, I haven't told her anything. She's a seer like I am."

Katova recaptures my attention. "The next card represents the difficulties or opposing forces in your life. It is A Curuxa, the barn owl. It represents death and darkness. It is also transmutation. The ordeal you are going through may seem like death, but you are being transformed, if you chose to accept the transformation. Remember you have free will." She gives me an inquiring look.

My heart is pounding, and my stomach clenches.

"The next card, the environmental influence exerting itself on you, is 'O Dragon,' the dragon, an ally of the druids. It is thought to be female and very powerful. I'm glad to see this card." She pauses again, appraising me. "You have the soul of a dragon. You are more powerful than you know or believe."

I exhale in relief. I didn't know I had been holding my breath.

"The fourth card is what is providing you help."

It's a woman sitting at a table with potions. There's a bookcase in the background full of jars.

"It is 'A Menciñeria,' the medicine woman, the healer. She is already helping you."

I nod. Helen.

"The fifth card summarizes what is transpiring now. 'As Lumias,' which is half goat and half woman and very lustful. You have a strong sexual connection with a man who is deceiving you. It is imperative that you learn the difference between love and lust." She raises her eyebrow at me.

The heat of a blush runs from my toes to the top of my head.

"The sixth and last card is the path ahead."

I know what this is.

"'O Labirinto,' the labyrinth. The problem you have can take away your energy or help you find the best solution. You have a tough road ahead. You found your way in, and now you will have to find your way out. You will have to do it by yourself, but you will never be alone. Call on your resources. They are there to help, but you must ask." She gives me a moment to digest all that she has said. "Please give me another card."

Using my left hand, I hand her a card. She places it on top of the labyrinth.

"This is 'A figa.'" A powerful feminine symbol against the evil eye," she says.

There is clearly relief in her voice.

"Another card. 'O Arresponsador,' are people who can help you find what you have lost and protect you from violence. You have a lot of powerful protection. But this is a very powerful lesson you are learning. She leans back in her chair and looks me over with concern. "You are a beautiful and naive young woman. Naiveté does not become you or protect you. You must be brutally honest with yourself to move through the situation. You must seek support from powerful women to teach you. It will not be easy, this mess that you have created through your choices."

I'm not sure I can take any more of this.

Her gaze moves to the upper left of the room. She smiles at me with understanding.

"But isn't that what we are here to do, to learn? We all make mistakes, create messes, and we learn from them."

I feel a modicum of relief.

She collects all the cards and puts them back in their box. "Life is not easy, and you have chosen a particularly hard path. But this, too, will pass." She stands and announces that it's time for dinner.

We walk back to the house, and she invites us to sit at the dining room table. She brings in dishes and silverware. I get up to offer help, but she motions for me to sit.

"This is my pleasure," she says.

Next, she brings in a cauldron of soup, fresh bread, olive

oil and serves our plates. She fills our glasses with wine and even brings a bone for Maeloc, who takes it to a corner to chew on.

I'm sharing a room with Brigit, and the boys are upstairs in the attic. Maeloc has been remanded to the barn.

I spend an uneasy night tossing and turning.

. . .

I'm awake early and ready to go. Katova stops me at the end of the driveway as the Dorans head on down the road.

"When you get to Santiago, you must purchase a figa made of jet. They are everywhere. Google the meaning and wear it constantly for protection. The scarf is protecting you until you get there."

A small spring is at the side of the road close to her property. I take a moment and sit by the stream, trying to process all I have learned. I have deluded myself. This thing with Chase is not over, not by a long shot. But I take comfort in knowing that Helen, Emily, and even Mom have my back. I get up and lean into the mountain that will take me to the top of the Galician Plateau.

The Dorans seem to know I need time alone and have not allowed me to catch up with them. I wonder if they think I really did allow myself to be filmed in the nude. Maybe they don't want anything to do with me.

I reflect back on the reading. It sure seems like I brought all this on myself. I remember feeling so sexy around him. He responded, then I acted like the virgin I am and pushed him away. One of my friends back home told me the best way to get a man is to push him away. Make him work for it. Well, I definitely was making Chase work for it in more ways than one. I'm as much to blame for the situation as he is.

I honestly enjoyed talking into the camera and making those videos. I knew I looked hot in the outfits I was wearing, and I could see it in his eyes. It's not the first time men have looked at me like that.

It's so frustrating. A woman is either a virgin or a whore. There's no in-between. I just want to be equal and respected in a relationship. Part of me believed that was where I was going with Chase – being a partner in his business. Helping him make money and grow his following. Is there anything wrong with that? I scoff – nothing, as long as I keep my clothes on. Oh God, how do I fix this?

The Dorans are sitting on the grass at the top of the mountain. Maeloc is sniffing along the side of the fence. I think I'll keep on walking.

Lugh calls my name. I can either pretend I didn't hear it or respond. Well, ignorance is what got me where I am.

What did Katova say? I must be brutally honest. I stop and turn.

"Come, sit and join us for lunch," Lugh says.

I join them and put my pack on the ground. I then offer them some of my snacks. They wave me off and munch on what they have.

Brigit breaks the silence. "Our mom is a menciñeiro. She will help you when we get to Santiago."

"I can't put my problems on your family. You've been so kind." I take a deep breath. "Besides, I'm so embarrassed. How did I allow this to happen?"

"You said you never took your clothes off. Were you telling me the truth?" Cú asks.

"Yes. I mean, no, I never took my clothes off. Yes, I am telling you the truth. But I did strut my stuff. I kind of asked for it."

"Uh, I don't think so," Lugh says. "We all flirt and strut our stuff, even guys. That doesn't mean we want our bodies plastered nude all over the internet. I mean," he puffs out his chest and strikes a pose, "I look pretty hot without my shirt, but I sure don't want you to take pictures of me without my pants on."

We all break into laughter.

"There's a middle ground between a Madonna and a whore," Cú chimes in. "You just have to find it."

"Now, where did that come from?" I ask.

"Sometimes we only see things in black and white. There are many shades of color in between." He stands up and brushes himself off.

This family is getting scarier by the moment. They can read minds.

"Remember, we are of Celtic blood," Lugh says.

I don't even know how to respond. We gather our trash and put it in our packs.

We pass through Abadín and head to As Paredes. The Camino takes us on a frontage road beside the main A8 highway that goes east to west across Spain. We go into the gate at the albergue, and the hospitalero says that someone will have to camp out with the dog, but the rest can stay inside. Lugh volunteers, and we stop for the night.

. . .

We begin the day walking alongside the highway to Vilalba. It's early when we arrive at the ancient town with a round tower. The tower is now connected to the parador. A parador is part of a hotel chain that refurbishes ancient buildings into high-dollar rooms. There is no way we can get in to see the tower. And there is no way I can put this experience on my credit card. We consult our guides.

The next town with a place to stay is Baamonde, eighteen kilometers away, which will make our walk today over thirty-three kilometers. We can do this.

We stop at the grocery store to dispose of trash and stock up on food. As we head out of town, Brigit starts singing 'Ultreia.' The road flattens out on the plateau, and walking is easy. Many fields flank the road, and the crops soak up the sun.

Every now and then, Brigit stops and picks a clover. They grow wild all along the road. I catch up with her and watch her carefully construct a necklace by making a slit in the stem of one and threading the stem of the next through the slit. I try, and soon we have two clover necklaces.

It's a rather uneventful rest of the day and we hit the Municipal albergue in Baamonde. I could do with a few more low-drama days. Maeloc is once again made to stay outside.

. . .

On the outskirts of Baamonde, we follow a road beside a railroad track. Brigit suddenly stops at a way marker with a plaque.

She reads it to us. "One hundred more kilometers to Santiago."

We drop our packs and take a moment to celebrate.

Cú does a handstand, and Lugh grabs his legs, making an arch over the marker. I snap their picture. Brigit takes her now-dried clover necklace and drapes it over the marker. I take mine from around my neck and do the same. We then make a heart with our hands over the marker, and Lugh snaps our picture.

"We have to have a picture of all four of us," Lugh says. We line up for a selfie with the marker. These will be great to post.

We're almost there. I laugh when I think back to planning this trip. One hundred kilometers was all I thought I could manage, and here I've already walked over seven times that distance. It blows my mind.

We come to a junction in the road and decide to take the alternate route to Parga. The alternate route, 'por A Cruces,' (by the crosses) cuts eight kilometers off the Camino, bypassing the town of Miraz. There is no reason to walk further than we have to.

The road winds through fields bursting with green crops. There are gentle ups and downs, but nothing like we have seen in the past. The walking is easy and fast. However, road-walking is taking its toll on Maeloc. We come upon an albergue in the small town of Praga. We have to rest. They have beds and food—a win-win.

Maeloc's booties are definitely worn. Brigit and I

brainstorm. The hospitalero gives us some fabric, and we make small cushions to put in the sole of each bootie. This should help. From here to Santiago, we'll be walking mostly on roads.

The hospitalero offers dinner and breakfast, and we can order a bag lunch for tomorrow as there will be no place to eat until we get to Sobrado Dos Monixes.

The rhythm of laundry, eating, sleeping, and walking soothes my soul. The hospitaleros—true to their name—tend to my needs, granting me the freedom to simply exist. I should savor it while I can, but the looming reality of facing up to my mistakes in Santiago lingers like a shadow, weighing heavily on my mind.

CHAPTER 15

PARGA TO DE SANTIAGO DE COMPOSTELA

Maeloc barking wakes me up out of a deep slumber. I turn over and the sun is streaming through the window. I quickly take care of my morning toilet, then walk out of our small cabin. Maeloc and Lugh are playing catch. I smile and wave, then head over to breakfast. There is a cardboard box on the table full of lunch bags. I grab the one with my name.

We once again find ourselves on an asphalt road. Lugh has Maeloc on a long leash. There are infrequent cars, and we step to the side to let them pass.

The town of Sobrado dos Monxes is bigger than most of the small hamlets we have been walking through. Its centerpiece is the Monastery of Santa Maria de Sobrado, which the guidebook says was originally built in 951 AD.

Wow, 951 AD, and they're still using it, though it has a long history of being abandoned and rebuilt over the years. It's obvious they are renovating the Cathedral's face next to the monastery.

We enter the cloister from a large green space. There are benches, and we are asked to sit until our turn to check-in. Only four pilgrims are allowed to check in at a time. This is quite a formal procedure. We are ushered into the office. Our credentials are checked and stamped. We pay eight euros each and collect our paper sheets and pillowcases.

Once again, Maeloc is not welcome. Cú takes his turn in roughing it to be with Maeloc. The rest of us are shown to a room off the open cloister. The showers and toilets are at one end of the cloister, and the washing machines at the other. The monk tells us that Vespers will be at seven p.m., and we're invited to attend. He informs us that the monastery door is locked at ten p.m. and will not open until six a.m. He's quite stern. There will be no pushing the boundaries with this guy.

Lugh and Brigit get cleaned up and hand me their laundry and Cú's clothes. It's so much cheaper and faster to share a load. They head out to check on Cú and Maeloc. I start the washer, set a timer, and go exploring.

I wander through the cloister, reading the plaques. I take a staircase to a side entrance into the Cathedral. The nave is an empty shell. I've never been in a church without pews or stations of the cross, and there is no statue or crucifix behind the altar. But there is something very moving about this huge empty space. It's as if God's presence filling it is enough. I look at the stonework and peek into every alcove. The stone is there for the altar, and I acknowledge its presence.

The emptiness of the space could allow it to be used for any type of worship. I picture Muslims with their prayer rugs, and this morphs into a pagan offering of herbs and flowers on the altar. I imagine people dancing in honor of spirit. It could even be a theater for artistic expression.

I'm getting a little off the traditional base. I'm not sure my priest back home would agree, but aren't we all worshiping the same thing, a divine presence? We just put our own cultural stamp on it. Why can't a large holy space exist where people can unite and celebrate the divine? I wonder how my father's family worships in Kenya. Maybe one day I'll find out.

It's like the threads of the scarf. I take it from my neck. All the different colors and beliefs are woven together to make a wondrous, supportive whole. I wish we as a people could do the same. Instead of fighting over our gods, we could come together in peace.

I check the time. It's getting close to Vespers. I make my way back out of the cathedral and into the cloister. A group is forming at the bottom of a roped-off stone staircase. Lugh waves me over to join a small group of chatting pilgrims.

One of the pilgrims, a tall man with a British accent, tells about lying down in a field to take a nap and dreaming about a beautiful girl he had seen along the way. In his dream, she kisses him. He then awakens and realizes that he is still lying in the field, and a cow is licking his face.

This hits Brigit's funny bone, and she starts to giggle. It's infectious. I can just picture it, and I legit lose it. My laughter explodes out of me like a whole sitcom laugh track.

The monk who checked us in comes over and admonishes us for being too loud. He reminds us that we are going into chapel. The man with a British accent looks directly at him.

"Are you really a monk?"

I bite my cheek to keep from breaking out into peals of laughter again. There is no way I can look at Brigit.

The monk draws himself up bigger in his black robes and speaks with an equally thick British accent. "Of course, I'm a monk. What do I look like? A bloody gorilla."

I nearly die. I cross my legs to prevent wetting my pants. The monk walks away from us, takes out a cigarette, and lights it. I can't stand it. I look at Brigit. She grabs my hand and squeezes it tightly, doing everything she can to avoid falling on the floor laughing.

Another monk comes down the steps and removes the barrier, and the group starts climbing the stairs to the chapel. I take some deep breaths, and Brigit does the same. We regain some semblance of control as we enter the chapel.

The service is lovely, and the monks' voices as they sing vespers are otherworldly. After they finish, we make our way out of the chapel. I run and throw the clothes in the dryer. We then head down to the square just outside the monastery for a bite to eat before bedtime.

"Remember the door is locked at ten p.m., not a second later," Brigit says, mimicking the British accent of the monk.

Cú is sitting at an outside table with Maeloc beside him. We join them. Cú tells us the pizza looks good and is shareable. We order pizza and beer. Cú says that he and Maeloc have found a private place to shelter for the night.

The British guy joins us, along with a couple of other pilgrims. He looks me straight in the eye and says, "What do I look like, a bloody gorilla?"

I spray my sip of beer all over the table, and the hysteria begins. It's one story after another. Someone checks the time, and we have less than ten minutes to pay the bill and get back to the cloister.

The monk stands at the gate, ready to lock it as we run up. He glares at us but lets us in. I collect our dry laundry and hand it out. Lugh takes Cú's clean clothes.

· · ·

Bells ring to call the monks to prayers. Morning already. I put the pillow over my head.

"Come on, sleepy head," Brigit says.

I roll out of bed and get ready for the day. We meet Cú and Maeloc at a little cafe and discuss our route options over coffee and tomato toast. We can take the Camino to Arzua and meet up with the Frances route, or we can take an older route and end up further west. We take a vote and Arzua wins.

We walk into Arzua, and the streets are teaming with pilgrims. There were pilgrims on the Norte, but this is ridiculous. We find an albergue for the second-to-last night on the Camino. It's huge, with laundry and cooking facilities. There's also a strong Wi-Fi signal. I post on Instagram that we will walk into Santiago the day after tomorrow. We grab food at a grocery store and make a simple dinner.

There's a text from the police in Gijón telling me to check in with the police when I reach Santiago. I had just about forgotten all about Chase and the videos. I acknowledge his message. It's back to reality for me.

· · ·

We walk out of town with a group of high school students from Barcelona. This is part of their curriculum. Can you imagine walking the Camino as part of your schoolwork?

A bus transports their packs. They look so free, playing and teasing each other. Their energy is contagious.

I've reached the point where I barely notice the pack I'm carrying. We surge towards Santiago, keeping up with the students. The fitness and strength I have gained blow my mind. I never thought I could do this. It feels so good.

We stop at the sound of bagpipes. There's a small crowd surrounding a man playing. He has an open case in front of him for donations. He completes a song and the British pilgrim from last night starts a conversation with him. He hands his bagpipes to the Brit and the Brit plays a few notes to get the feel of it. He starts to tap a slow rhythm out with his foot. The first few notes of Amazing Grace slide out of the pipes. It's spellbinding. Brigit begins to sing the words in a clear voice, and I join her. Pretty soon, everyone is singing Amazing Grace. Tears roll down my face.

The last note fades away, and we break into applause. The Brit hands the pipes back to the piper and throws a donation into the case. We all dig for coins and share them. I hope he gets a good meal and a place to stay. I have heard that many people live on the Camino and survive on donations alone.

Hours later, we are herded into a huge albergue in O Pedrouzo, with one hundred and twenty beds. We feel lucky to have one. Lugh stays outside with Maeloc.

. . .

I wake up rested. Only nineteen more kilometers to go. The Dorans and I merge back into the flow of pilgrims, frequently passing cafes and booths of people selling Camino souvenirs. Once again, we start to climb. It's our last hill, the Monte de Gozo, the Mountain of Joy. My heart is full.

At the top, there is a chapel and a grassy mound. We sit on the mound. Santiago spreads out below us. I can just make out the spires of the cathedral in the distance. It's still five more kilometers to the Cathedral.

We share snacks one last time and Brigit texts her mom to let her know we are on our way in. I wish my mom and my dad in heaven were here to celebrate this with me. Tears come into my eyes.

"Vamos," Lugh says. We clean up our snacks and shoulder our packs one last time.

The Camino leads us through the modern part of the city, where we stop at a colorful sign that says 'Santiago' and we take pictures. Deeper into the city, the new becomes the old. We cross a modern thoroughfare and enter the narrow cobblestone streets of the old part of town. I believe this is the longest five kilometers of the entire Camino.

We turn the final corner, and the great Plaza de Obradoiro spreads out before us. It's a huge stone area surrounded by ancient buildings, with the Cathedral facing it. Hundreds of pilgrims are celebrating. Brigit, Cú, and Lugh grab me for a group hug, and Maeloc noses his way into the middle of the circle. I bend down and give him a hug too.

A woman is yelling, and it's their mom. Their mom and dad have come to celebrate their accomplishment. I step aside.

"Valerie!" Carl is coming across the plaza towards me. I run to him, and we hug.

He takes a step back. "Congratulations, you made it." He looks around. "Did you ghost Chase again?"

"He's not with me, and it's a long story. " Remembering this puts a damper on my celebration.

"I'm glad," Carl says.

I wonder if he knew something was up with Chase and just never said anything.

Brigit gives me a questioning look, separates herself from her family, and walks over to join us. Her family follows her. She introduces me to her parents, and I introduce Carl as a friend whom I walked with early on in my pilgrimage. I explain that I haven't seen him since Güemes. It's amazing that we would see each other in Santiago.

"Come on, let's go to the Pilgrims' office to get your Compostelas," her mother says, leading the way.

We put our information into the kiosk, get a number, and

join the line. Brigit sidles up to me and says, "You can also get a Compostela in the name of someone you walked for."

I smile and when I reach the desk, I get a Compostela for myself and one in my father's name. He has been with me the entire way in the form of the doll he gave me as a child. It's only right to honor him.

"Let's go eat," Brigit's mom suggests. "I've fixed a lovely meal for all of you." She makes it known that her offer includes me and Carl.

But Carl makes his excuses. He's promised Ana that he will meet her for lunch. I wink at him, and we exchange contact information. The rest of us make our way through town to the Doran's home. Maeloc is so happy to be let loose in his own backyard. It's a lovely meal.

"Now rest. We must go to the evening pilgrims' mass. I have it on good authority that the botafumeiro is going to fly," Mrs. Doran says with a wink.

"What's a botafumeiro?" I ask.

"You will see," she says. "Now go rest."

I settle into my bed in the room I share with Brigit. I call Mom, and she answers on the first ring.

"I made it. I'm in Santiago and staying with the Dorans. They are so nice."

"I knew you could do it," she says.

My chest swells with pride.

A man in the background asks my mother who is on the phone.

"It's Valerie. She's safe in Santiago," Mom replies.

The man says, "I knew she would make it. She's your daughter."

"Who's that?"

"A friend of your father's from Kenya. He's here in Florida on business and wanted to visit."

"Someone from Kenya?"

"Yes, it's a long story. I'll explain when you get home,"

"Are you sure he's on the up and up?" The bad taste Chase left in my mouth is making me fear for my mom.

"Yes, he's safe. Your grandparents called with an introduction. We'll talk all about it when you get home."

Whoa, Mom has a guy from Kenya at the house. I wonder what this is all about.

I smile and post our celebration pictures on Facebook and Instagram. Dot immediately responds with a GIF of congratulations, and then my other friends chime in. I text the policeman in Gijón to tell him that I have arrived in Santiago. He gives me the name and number of the local policeman handling the case. I then call and let them know where I am staying.

In need of a siesta after all this excitement, I lay down and shut my eyes. It feels like only moments have passed and I'm woken up by noise elsewhere in the house. I get up and dress and make my way downstairs.

"Vamos, Valerie. We have to get to mass," Cú says.

We return to the Cathedral and find a seat close to the altar. At the end of mass, a group of men in burgundy robes, ascends to the presbytery in front of the altar.

Mr. Doran leans over and whispers in my ear, "They are called 'tiraboleiros.' They will swing the botafumeiro. The incense burner. The incense covers the smell of stinky pilgrims."

Each man holds a rope attached to a central long rope, from which hangs a huge silver incense burner. The priest lights the incense and starts it swinging. The tiraboleiros pull on their ropes in unison, and the botafumeiro soars up to the cathedral's ceiling. As they pull in rhythm, it flies through the transcript, emitting scented smoke over the pilgrims.

I watch in amazement. Too soon, it is caught and pulled back to its resting place. With the final strains of the organ, we exit the church.

"Tomorrow afternoon we come back to visit the saint and take the rooftop tour," Mrs. Doran says. "I must go to the shop in the shop. In the morning. Would you like to join me, Valerie?"

"Yes ma'am, I'd like that very much."

When I return to my room, I check my phone. The local police have left a message: Chase Damon has been extradited to the United States to stand trial. We have provided your contact information to the receiving authorities, who will get in touch with you.

The tarot cards are correct. It's not over yet, but at least I don't have to deal with it until I get home. There's going to be a lot to deal with when I get home. But I know I have the strength to confront it head on.

. . .

After breakfast, Mrs. Doran and I go to her shop. It's in the old part of the city, only a couple of blocks from the cathedral. It's filled with healing herbs, jewelry, statues, and crystals. There are also some postcards and Camino swag.

She beckons me to a case containing scallop shells and fists made from a black stone she calls azabache, also known as jet. She explains that it is a type of amber used to make sacred jewelry. From the case, she pulls out a black fist with a silver ring on the end which is attached to a silver chain. She unhooks the chain and puts it around my neck.

"Is it a figa?" I ask.

"Yes, it will protect you." She explains that the figa wards off the evil eye. The fist has the thumb protruding between the first and second fingers. This symbol represents the power of the woman, symbolizing the labia and the clitoris.

A blush comes over my cheeks. Women's genitals.

"Katova told me I needed to buy one."

"Katova is very wise." She gently touches the fringe of the scarf. "This scarf has protected you, but you must pass it on. You will need something else to protect you going forward. I could see it the moment I laid eyes on you. You are struggling. If you want to talk about it, I am here."

I reach for my purse, not knowing if I can afford something so precious.

She closes her hand around mine.

"This is my gift to you, woman to woman. Let's go grab a cup of coffee and talk."

We find a table in a quiet corner of the coffee shop. The kindness on Mrs. Doran's face breaks me open. The shame spills out before I can stop it—the lies I told my mother, the way I let myself get swept up by Chase.

"I'm such a loser," I whisper.

She reaches across the table and takes my hand, her touch warm and steady. "Oh, my child, you are not a loser. You are worthy. You are innocent. You will always be so. You may not feel it now, but one day, you will look back on this time and smile." She pauses as if waiting for the weight of her words to settle in my heart. "Let me tell you the two truths of the universe. Write them down, keep them close, and return to them whenever you need them."

I pull out my phone, fingers trembling, and prepare to type.

"Everything happened in the only way it could have. And everyone did the best they could with what they knew and with what they had available at the time—physically, emotionally, mentally, and spiritually. Everyone. Every time. Period."

She waits a second then takes the end of my scarf and dabs my damp cheeks. "You are too young to carry such a heavy burden. Release it, my dear. And when you're ready— *DANCE.*"

The journey of the scarf continues in Book Three with Dot, the wise Crone. Keep reading for a sneak peek ...

BOOK III

THINK LIKE THE CRONE

Dot

Love like the Mother
Dance like the Maiden
Think like the Crone

- Stenciled on a jar of homemade Sangria
that was given to me by a wise crone.

CHAPTER I

HOME TO LISBON

"Dot, it was such a lovely funeral," the hospice nurse says as she gives me a hug.

"I'm so grateful for your support. I couldn't have kept Hal home without you." I smile and when she steps to her left to speak to my daughter I turn to the next mourner in line. I'm also grateful for the shade of the tent as the hot summer southern California shine beats down on us.

After my daughter and I speak to all the guests, we drive home for the funeral lunch.

"Mom, did you do the deviled eggs?"

"Of course I did, darling. They're in the refrigerator in the garage."

That child of mine is micromanaging everything, but I don't know how I would have gotten through the past several years without her.

In need of a moment, I go upstairs to what used to be 'our' bedroom and sit on the rocker by the now-empty bed. I've spent many hours here. Out of habit, I pick up my cell phone and check Facebook. So many wonderful old friends are reaching out to me.

A notice from Valerie. I've become hooked on following her Camino. Fresh energy, a youth on an adventure. Just what I need. I still recall all the adventures of my youth. I'm not ready to hang up the hiking shoes yet.

I scroll my feed and there she is, waving that beautiful scarf over her head in front of the Cathedral in Santiago. I'm as proud of her as I would be of my own grandchild, and I've never met her. I send a GIF of congratulations.

Karen calls up to me. "Mom, the guests are arriving."

Downstairs, I see the wonderful family and friends we've collected over the years. They've been with us every step of the way. It's hard to imagine that a brilliant mind like Hal's would succumb to Alzheimer's. It was horrible watching him die inch by inch.

Hal's brother, Charlie, grabs me and gives me a bear hug. "So Dot, what are your plans now?"

"I'm going to walk the Camino," I say, surprising myself.

The room quiets. Karen restrains her brother.

"It's just the grief talking," she whispers to him. But I hear. A mother always hears.

"No, really. I've given this much thought, and I know I can do it. I'm going to walk to Santiago." I must've been giving this a lot of thought and didn't realize I was serious until now.

Karen puts her arm around my shoulder as if she's the mom and I'm the daughter. She addresses the crowd. "Thank you all for coming. It means so much to Mom and the family. You took care of us while Dad was sick. Let us take care of you today. After Father Francis asks the blessing we'll have lunch. It's a buffet starting at this end of the table. We have tables and chairs set up on the lanai. Just find a place to sit. There's an open bar with both non-alcoholic and alcoholic beverages. Enjoy."

"Please bow your heads," Father says.

I'm ashamed to say that I don't even hear the blessing. My mind jumps back to the Camino and that picture of Valerie in front of the Cathedral. Her joy transcends the space between us and settles in my soul.

Ribadedeva, Camino del Norte

ALDER ALLENSWORTH

Alder Allensworth began her career as a therapist and continues her work in healing as a nurse, helping people navigate life's challenges. In 2017, she walked her first Camino—the Frances. While in Burgos, she received news that her manuscript, *Prevail: Celebrate the Journey*, had won a publishing contract with Richter Publishing. The book was released in 2018.

In 2022, she returned to the Camino for a writer's retreat, where the seeds of this trilogy began to take shape. In a moment of serendipity, a long-lost scarf found its way back to her. She carried it to the top of O'Cebreiro, where she captured the image that now graces the cover of Book One.

Alder continued her pilgrimage in 2024, walking the Camino Norte. Her journeys—both personal and professional—have been dedicated to healing, resilience, and transformation. She is an active member of the Tampa Writers Alliance and a dedicated advocate for Alzheimer's awareness. Alongside her partner, Brenda Freed, she co-authored *Mackenzie Meets Alzheimer's Disease*, a picture book designed to help children understand the condition. Together, they developed the *Mackenzie Meets Alzheimer's Awareness Program* to support families navigating dementia.

Passionate about the Camino and the power of healing journeys, Alder is deeply involved with *American Pilgrims on the Camino*.

She lives in Tampa, Florida, and can be contacted through her website www.alderallensworth.com/ or directly by email at aldertree0720@gmail.com.

www.ingramcontent.com/pod-product-compliance
Lightning Source LLC
Chambersburg PA
CBHW020415260626
47156CB00007B/2404